Laziness Detox

Cleansing Bad Habits to Boost Productivity

PRIYANSHU JAIN

PRABHAT
PRAKASHAN

Published by
PRABHAT PRAKASHAN PVT. LTD.
4/19 Asaf Ali Road,
New Delhi-110 002 (INDIA)
e-mail: prabhatbooks@gmail.com

ISBN 978-93-5562-808-4
Laziness Detox: Cleansing Bad Habits to Boost Productivity
by Priyanshu Jain

Edition
First, 2024

Price
₹ 350.00 (Rupees Three Hundred Fifty only)

Printed at
Sita Fine Arts, Delhi

Author's Note

When I embarked on the journey of writing this book, I had no idea how profoundly it would impact my own life. The research and self-exploration required to create it forced me to confront my own struggles with procrastination, lack of motivation and unproductive habits head-on.

Through this process, I have come to realise that laziness is not a character flaw or a personality trait, but rather a manifestation of deeply ingrained patterns and thought processes that can be rewired. It is a cycle that feeds upon itself, but one that can be broken with the right tools and mindset shifts.

In this book, you will find practical strategies, psychological insights and actionable steps to help you identify and overcome the root causes of your unproductive behaviours. But more than that, this book is a call to embrace a lifestyle of intentionality, discipline and purpose.

My hope is that by sharing my own experiences and the wisdom gathered from experts in various fields, I can help you reclaim your time, energy and motivation, allowing you to live up to your full potential.

Remember, this journey is not about perfection, but about progress. Every small step you take towards breaking free from the shackles of laziness and inertia is a victory worth celebrating.

Embrace the discomfort, lean into the challenges and let this book be your guide towards a more fulfilling, productive and purposeful life.

Acknowledgement

I am profoundly grateful to everyone who supported and inspired me throughout the journey of writing this book on detoxing life. This work is a culmination of my experiences, research, and dedication to promoting a healthier, more balanced lifestyle amidst the chaos of modern professional life.

First and foremost, I would like to thank my family and friends for their unwavering support and encouragement. Your belief in my vision has been the cornerstone of this project. To my mentors and colleagues, your insights and feedback have been invaluable in shaping the content and direction of this book.

I extend my heartfelt gratitude to the readers. Your journey towards a detoxed and balanced life is the ultimate reward for my efforts. I hope this book serves as a guiding light, helping you to cultivate these practices and transform your life.

Thank you for allowing me to be a part of your wellness journey.

Contents

Author's Note 3

Acknowledgement 5

The Laziness Trap

Chapter 1 What Makes Us Lazy? 11

Chapter 2 Exploring Brain Patterns (Neuroscience) 15

Chapter 3 The Psychology of Procrastination 20

Chapter 4 Laziness or Depression? 26

The Habits That Stick

Chapter 5 Comfort Zone – Our Enemy 33

Chapter 6 Fear of Failure 37

Chapter 7 Perfectionism 42

Chapter 8 Decision Paralysis 47

Chapter 9 Parkinson's Law 51

Mindful Practices

Chapter 10 Enabling Growth 59

Chapter 11 Self-Compassion 62

Chapter 12 Motivation 67
Chapter 13 Discipline 71
Chapter 14 Outcomes 76
Chapter 15 Objectivity 82

Healthy Practices

Chapter 16 You Are What You Eat 89
Chapter 17 Exercise Most Days 96
Chapter 18 Sleep Well 101
Chapter 19 Moments of Bliss 107
Chapter 20 Set Reasonable Goals 114
Chapter 21 Create Accountability 121
Chapter 22 Create an Action Plan 125
Chapter 23 Tech Time-Out (Digital Detox) 130
Chapter 24 Meditation 136

Time Management Techniques

Chapter 25 The Eisenhower Matrix 145
Chapter 26 Kaizen's Philosophy 150
Chapter 27 Pomodoro Technique 156
Chapter 28 Pareto Analysis 161
Chapter 29 Eat that Frog Technique 167

Sum Up

Chapter 30 Wake Up Before It is Too Late 173

The Laziness Trap

CHAPTER 1
What Makes Us Lazy?

"The way we spend our time defines who we are."
– Jonathan Estrin

We've all been there – lounging on the couch, binge-watching our favourite show or doing nothing and putting off or delaying that important task or project we know we should be working on. Laziness is a universal human experience, and it can be a real productivity killer. But what exactly makes us lazy in the first place?

Well, there are actually a few different factors at play. First, there is the biological aspect. Our brains are hardwired to conserve energy whenever possible through what is known as the "law of least effort." This evolutionary mechanism served our ancient ancestors well – back in caveman days, you didn't want to waste precious calories on unnecessary activities when you might need that energy to hunt for food or fleeing from predators. Resting and avoiding strenuous work made sound survival sense.

But in today's world of modern convenience and abundant resources, this innate tendency towards sloth can backfire evidently. With temptations like comfortable sofas, ready-to-eat foods and unlimited entertainment at our fingertips, it is all too easy to succumb to inertia. Our bodies and brains still crave to conserve energy, even when physical exertion is no longer a matter of life-or-death.

Take something as simple as walking up a flight of stairs versus taking the elevator. Your body will naturally push you towards the path of least resistance (the elevator) because from an evolutionary standpoint, why waste energy on stair-climbing if you don't have to? But giving in to these subtle lazy impulses day after, can lead to seriously sedentary lifestyles.

Then there is the psychological side of laziness. Procrastination is perhaps the most obvious mental barrier to productivity. We all know that sinking feeling of putting something off even though we know we'll pay for it later with more stress and rushed work. But procrastination is a hard habit to break because it's driven by very real psychological factors like task resistance, lack of motivation, fear of failure and poor self-regulation.

Let's say you have an important research paper to write for class. Just thinking about the depth of research, writing, and editing involved can make you want to run and hide under your covers. This "task aversion" stems from your brain trying to avoid anything it perceives as too difficult or unpleasant. And the more you visualise the pain of working on that paper now, the more you will want to procrastinate to make those bad feelings go away...at least temporarily.

Perfectionism is another major form of procrastination in disguise. You might delay getting started on a project because you are paralysed by the desire to do it perfectly from the outset. Rather than making incremental progress and adjusting as you go, your perfectionist mentality tricks you into believing you must have every tiny detail figured out before you can begin. Which rarely, if ever happens, results in chronic procrastination?

Fear of failure is yet another driver of laziness. If you are terrified of not living up to expectations or of "messing up," you may subconsciously avoid putting yourself in situations where you could fail. Sticking to your comfort zone and the status quo, even if underwhelming could start to feel safer than risking failure through actions.

Our habits and surroundings also heavily influence how lazy we are. If we have fallen into a pattern of sedentary behaviour – spending lots of time sitting, frequently snacking, not incorporating much physical activity – our bodies and minds become accustomed to that low energy state. Making it increasingly harder to overcome inertia and get moving.

Our social circles and communities also play a role. If we are surrounded by people who are leading active, ambitious lives and checking off goals left and right, we are more likely to be influenced by their energy and example. But if our friends and family are chronically lazy or actively enabling of those lazy tendencies, it becomes an uphill and tough battle.

Then there are larger, societal forces that can promote cultures of laziness – like the rise of labour-saving devices that remove the "need" for physical effort, or metaphysical beliefs that valorise concepts like Santosham paraṃ sukham (ultimate bliss is satisfaction). Not to mention value system that prioritises wealth, status and consumption over constructive output.

The perpetual lure of new streaming shows, video games and other entertainment options enabled by technology doesn't help either. Why do anything productive when you can effortlessly escape into virtual realms or be an armchair sports spectator for hours on end?

And let's not forget the impact of mental and physical health issues that can drastically sap motivation and energy. From clinical depression and anxiety to chronic pain conditions like fibromyalgia, these internal factors can make something as simple as getting out of bed feel like running a marathon some days.

However, despite all these factors and forces, the path to overcoming laziness starts with this first step of self-awareness. Recognising which unique factors are feeding your lazy behaviours is crucial for addressing them head-on. Once you shine a light on the root causes, you can start making lasting and enduring changes. You have got the power to break free from the laziness trap. But it will take commitment, patience and willingness to experiment with new perspectives and routines.

❑

CHAPTER 2

Exploring Brain Patterns (Neuroscience)

"The brain is like a muscle. When it is in use we feel very good. Understanding is joyous."

– Carl Sagan

Have you ever stopped to wonder what is actually going on in your brain when those unproductive urges kick in and why are some people lazier than others? The human brain is a complex machine, performing countless calculations and neurological processes every second to keep us functioning. And many of those behind-the-scenes operations can directly impact how lazy or motivated we feel.

Let's start by exploring the key brain regions involved in motivation and goal-oriented behaviour. Meet the Pre-Frontal Cortex (PFC) – this is the cerebral "control centre" that handles high-level functions like decision-making, problem-solving and voluntary behaviour regulation. When you are feeling focused and driven to tackle a task, it is partially because of increased activity in the PFC. This brain area essentially puts on its "boss hat" and tells the rest of your brain "All right troops, we have got a mission – let's get it done!"

The PFC works closely with another crucial region called the Anterior Cingulate Cortex (ACC). This acts like a "cognitive control" filter, helping you bypass urges, distractions and knee-jerk impulses in order to stay locked on your goal. When activity in the PFC and ACC areas of the brain decreases, you lose that feeling of motivation and drive. However, other parts of the brain like the limbic system, which controls basic emotions and desires like seeking pleasure, then get a stronger influence. That's when you might suddenly feel an overwhelming urge to discard or give up that spread-sheet you were working on and instead watch entertaining YouTube videos.

The brain is a constant multi-ring circus of activity. There are all kinds of other neurological factors and chemical messengers that can tip you towards productivity or idleness. One major player is dopamine – a neurotransmitter that plays a key role in motivation, pleasure and reward-driven learning. Dopamine hits provide a tiny explosion of feel-good satisfaction, reinforcing whatever behaviour triggered that chemical reward. If you start feeling a lazy impulse and you give in, that minuscule burst of lazy-enabling dopamine can make you more likely to repeat that unhelpful behaviour in future. It is scary, creating a vicious, self-perpetuating cycle of idleness over time.

It is the same brain mechanism that can help build new, better habits when you constantly show up for them. Over time, the acts of working towards your goals become the path of least neurological resistance. But these neural patterns of laziness or drive don't just emerge from nowhere. A lot of it comes down to how our brains were "wired" from a young age based on our upbringings and life experiences.

See, the human brain remains remarkably malleable (a trait called Neuroplasticity) well into adulthood. Which means our habits and beliefs during childhood and adolescence exerted an enormous influence on how our motivational circuitry developed over time.

If you grew up in an environment surrounded by lazy, unmotivated influences – that may have become the predominant default setting your brain learned to operate in. Leaving you stuck in those entrenched patterns till you consciously reprogram them. On the other side, being raised by parents or role models who were productive and dynamic likely helped solidify more motivational brain wiring and reward pathways early on. That's not to say you are completely doomed by the cards you were dealt.

So, with all these opposing neural forces at play, how can we start tilting the playing field back towards productivity optimising our neurological wiring? Well, that mostly comes down to Hebb's principle of Neuroplasticity. It describes how connections between neurons in the brain are constantly being stubbed out or reinforced through "neurons that fire together, wire together" process based on our thoughts and behaviours. So while some of your current brain patterning around laziness may be rooted in your past circumstances and outdated neural pathways, you absolutely can rewrite those circuits through sustained, conscious effort.

It is like physical exercise – working out a muscle gradually strengthens it, building new connections. Apply that same principle to your desired motivational habits and mindsets, and you will start forging new motivational "musculature" in your brain. Don't just idly scroll through social media; set a timer and use it as a planned break reward only after you have cranked out that report for a while. Celebrate small victories and you are positively reinforcing the neuro-connections you want.

You know that feeling when you have been hyper-focused on an intense thinking task for hours, and you start to feel drained? That's because cerebrally-demanding activities requiring high PFC involvement can actually lead to temporary mental fatigue and motivation depletion. Your brain only has so much oxygenated glucose resources to go around at any given time. And the PFC is a particularly gluttonous, energy-hungry area. In these moments of depletion, the brain tends to shift to a more impulsive, distracted mode of operating. Ever notice how lethargic you might feel after mentally gruelling bouts of study or concentrated work? That's your lazy brain taking over temporarily until you are refuelled.

Getting sufficient sleep, exercise and nutrition helps to ensure the glucose tanks of your brain stay topped up for better stamina and motivation. Otherwise, your dopamine supplies can flame out faster. The more you engage in these seemingly minor yet persistent neural remapping, the stronger those fresh pathways and habits become hardwired into the fabric of your brain. Over time, the new productive mindsets and behaviours become your default operating setting, with laziness being the exception rather than the rule.

Of course, none of this brain remodelling happens overnight. It takes consistent discipline to continually exercise those motivational circuits through sustained, conscious repetition. The human brain is a remarkably adaptable and an ever-evolving landscape. You may not be able to fully control the inertia of deeply-ingrained lazy neurology you have inherited from your past conditioning. But you have the power to be purposeful architects of your motivational mindsets and habits going forward.

Stick with the process, keep showing up for yourself, and watch as your brain patterns steadily morph into sleeker, more energised, productive configurations. Optimised neural software begets optimised behavioural output. That is the magic of neuroplasticity!

❑

CHAPTER 3

The Psychology of Procrastination

Don't let procrastination take over your life. Be brave and take risks. Your life is happening right now.

– Roy Bennett

Staring down a looming deadline while finding weirdly creative ways to avoid the task at hand. Suddenly, clearing out your email inbox or reorganizing your closet becomes a top priority. Anything to stay in the comfortable realm of procrastination instead of buckling down, we have all been there. Procrastination is a near-universal experience.

Since it is so pervasive, you'd think there would be a simple, rational explanation for procrastination. But the more psychologists dig into why we procrastinate, the more complicated and fascinating the root causes become. It turns out procrastination is a deeply ironic behaviour – something we all know is going to make us feel worse in the long run, yet we still persist in doing it almost against our own self-interests.

On the surface, it may seem like laziness, lack of motivation, poor time management skills, or just general disorganisations are the main drivers of procrastination. And while those can certainly enable procrastination, psychologists have found the real core reasons are more complex and stem from our hard-wired human needs for emotional regulation.

Procrastination is what is known as a "maladaptive coping mechanism" in terms of psychology. It is a misguided attempt to avoid negative emotions and anxieties surrounding a particular task or goal in the short-term, despite the inevitably bigger pile of stress it creates later on.

For instance, let's say you have been assigned a huge research paper that's going to require extensive reading, writing, analysis, etc. Just the thought of tackling something so daunting and time-consuming makes your brain start spinning with doubts, insecurities and fears of failure. So in that moment of anxiety and task-aversion, procrastinating and distracting yourself with other activities provides a temporary emotional escape from those bad feelings. Your brain is essentially thinking "If I don't start this yet, I can't feel anxious or risk failing...at least for now."

Of course, we all know on a rational level that running from the task won't make it go away. In fact, it's only going to create more anxiety and stress when we are crunched for time at the deadline. But in that present moment, our brains latch onto instant gratification and relief.

Psychologists have identified several common "profiles" for the types of behaviours and thought patterns that tend to lead people into chronic procrastination:

- **The Worrier:** Continuously doubts their own abilities and competence, leading them to avoid starting tasks for fear they won't be able to successfully complete them. Their internal monologue is one of "I'm just going to mess this up, so why even begin?"

- **The Perfectionist:** Hold themselves to impracticably high standards and won't begin tasks unless they can do them flawlessly from the outset. Anything short of certain perfection feels like failure, so they would rather procrastinate than risk anything but perfection.
- **The Over-Doer:** Chronically take on too many commitments and responsibilities, but fails to properly prioritize them. So, while in constant motion, they rarely actually complete priority tasks on time.
- **The Crisis Maker:** Thrives on the adrenaline rush of last-minute panics and "fire drill" crunches against crazy deadlines. They actively procrastinate to create emergencies to feel motivated and focused.
- **The Dreamer:** Struggles with following through on tasks because concrete implementation feels tedious and boring. They would much rather stay in the ideation phase, convincing themselves the outcome will just magically happen.
- **The Defier:** The contrarian and rebel who procrastinates as an act of resistance to authority figures and having tasks imposed on them.

There are a plethora of other reasons why people procrastinate: low self-confidence, fear of not meeting expectations, avoiding difficult or unpleasant tasks, lacking motivation without immediate rewards and so on. But the uniting thread is procrastination being used as a coping mechanism to regulate moods and anxieties around tasks.

Interestingly, research shows procrastination isn't just correlated to lacking skills like time management, attention regulation, or self-control. Many procrastinators are actually highly capable and talented people who simply struggle to deploy those abilities consistently due to emotions and maladaptive coping styles. So while better productivity systems and motivation techniques can help minimize procrastination, at its core it really is a psychological issue of how we frame and react to tasks that provokes avoidance in the first place.

This is why Cognitive Behavioural Therapy (CBT) has proven to be an effective form of treatment for severely negatively impacted procrastinators. CBT helps people identify those unhelpful or unproductive thought patterns and develop healthier coping mechanisms through reframing their negative mental narratives. For example, worriers can learn to challenge beliefs about competence. Perfectionists can start separating self-worth from achievements. Over-Doers can work on priority management and saying "no" more often.

Another area psychologists are exploring is the role of our increasingly distraction-filled environments in enabling procrastination. With endless feeds of videos, games, social media, and other rapid-reward stimuli at our fingertips, it is easier than ever to escape into procrastination mode. Our brains are wired to crave those bursts of entertainment pleasure, sabotaging our good intentions through "just this one" rationalisations, until procrastination becomes the norm.

Similarly, psychologists note how cultural values like individualism and scepticism of authority can also feed into procrastination. If we grow up being taught to challenge rules and assert our independence, instructions from teachers, parents or managers can be subconsciously interpreted as impositions to resist. Other factors like negative mindsets ("I'm just lazy and unmotivated by nature"), self-handicapping behaviours, and even our sleep schedule and circadian habits can all shape our psychological relationships with procrastination over time.

The good news is that since procrastination stems from beliefs and coping styles we have learned, they can be unlearned and optimised through conscious effort, commitment and the right mental frame-working.

Serious procrastinators may benefit from working with therapists or coaches to dig into their core drivers and negative thought patterns around tasks. But many people can start re-wiring for less procrastination through simple self-awareness and metacognitive exercises. For instance, just taking a few minutes to pause and label the anxieties you are feeling around a particular task or deadline can help short-circuit the urge to procrastinate. Bringing tucked away sentiments into the forefront of consciousness makes you less likely to bury them through avoidance.

Creating concrete implementation plans with specific schedules and milestones for big projects can scratch that longing for perfectionists who procrastinate over wanting the perfect plan. For those who are threshold responders and only get motivated by impending panic, self-imposing reasonable-but-meaningful personal deadlines ahead of official ones can provide the pressure you crave while leaving more breathing room.

The overtaxed multitaskers out there, who procrastinate out of being overwhelmed, need learning to prioritize ruthlessly and say "no" more often in order to restore valuable headspace and attention. Use the "eat that frog" technique by tackling your biggest, prioritized to-do first each day before getting distracted.

While modern tech and environments have arguably made procrastination a little too tempting and easy, the human psychology behind it is a deep-rooted phenomenon. Beating that ingrained procrastination habit loop will take conscious reframing of our notion and behaviour towards tasks over time. But we are absolutely capable of optimizing our minds through commitment, self-study and determined practise.

No more falling into avoidance as a default coping mechanism! It is time to cultivate the motivational mindsets and self-assuring narratives we all deserve.

❑

CHAPTER 4

Laziness or Depression?

"The tragedy in life doesn't lie in not reaching your goal. The tragedy lies in having no goal to reach."

– Benjamin E. Mays

On the surface, laziness and depression can look pretty similar – low energy, lack of motivation, fatigue and difficulties in focusing on work or responsibilities. It is easy to get them confused or lump them together. But while lazy feelings and depression share some outward behaviour, they are ultimately different issues with distinct symptoms, solutions and root causes. Understanding the key differences is important for properly addressing whichever one you may be struggling with.

Laziness is a tendency to avoid effort whenever possible and take the easy way out – failing to live up to your full potential. It usually stems from things like poor self-discipline, fear of discomfort, lack of motivation or misaligned rewards and incentives. Depression, on the other hand, is a serious medical condition involving imbalanced brain chemistry that impacts your mood, energy levels, motivation and more. It causes persistent feelings of sadness, hopelessness, low self-worth and an inability to feel pleasure or joy no matter your life circumstances.

With laziness, even during our most unmotivated phases, we still tend to have relatively normal emotional ups and downs. Our core feelings about ourselves and sense of identity remain somewhat intact. We can still find happiness in hobbies, loved ones, positive life events and so on. But with clinical depression, you experience this heavy, overriding sense of emptiness, apathy and feeling disconnected from things you normally love. That profound emotional flatness is a red flag that something is metabolically out of balance in your brain and body.

People with depression also frequently experience very physical symptoms – disrupted sleep patterns, big appetite changes, unexplained aches and pains, feeling slowed down or "weighed down" and general fatigue. These embodied experiences go way beyond just lack of motivation from laziness.

Many depressed individuals struggle with something called Psychomotor Retardation – which makes every little action, thought process and decision feel utterly draining and hard. It is like trying to walk through dense fog mentally and physically all day, every day. The amount of effort required for basic self-care tasks like showering, eating regular meals or even getting out of bed can feel monumental in a way that regular laziness doesn't come close to. It is a whole-body depletion at a cellular level.

It is also crucial to understand that while laziness might increase some risk factors for future depression by allowing negative mindsets and isolation to fester, laziness itself doesn't directly cause clinical depression. There are many complex biological, genetic, life circumstance and other factors that can trigger depressive episodes. Things like family history of depression, major life stressors like loss or trauma, chronic health problems, seasonal patterns and more can all contribute to the onset of depression – not just being lazy.

That said, researches do suggest some potential overlapping brain mechanisms between laziness and depression; both seem to involve under activity in the Prefrontal Cortex (the brain's "control centre" for focus and goal-setting) and over activity in the brain's reward/pleasure-seeking hubs.

While laziness alone isn't causing depression, the two can create a self-perpetuating cycle where productive endeavours feel harder and harder as your brain gets stuck in patterns of motivational inertia and comfort cravings. A neural feedback loop forms making it tough to snap out of. But again, clinical depression is very much a medical condition requiring professional treatment – it's not something you can just "work harder" or "power through" with sheer will power and self-discipline alone.

So how can you tell if you are dealing with laziness or legitimate depression? One of the biggest distinctions is the severity and persistence of your symptoms over time.

We all cycle through periodic unmotivated inactive phases as a normal part of life. You might have felt particularly lazy for a week after a big life event, failure or transition. That is not necessarily depression. But if you have been experiencing severe, inescapable fatigue, persistent sadness, inability to derive any joy from previously valued activities, and majorly disrupted sleep and eating patterns for two weeks straight or longer – that's a red flag for likely clinical depression that warrants medical evaluation.

Getting in tune with the root causes and emotional "flavour" of your motivational struggles is necessary. If there's an acute, enveloping sense of darkness, emptiness and self-loathing disconnected from your circumstances that goes beyond typical laziness into depressive territory. So if you are battling that level of profound, hopeless-feeling inertia that feels entirely outside your control for weeks on end, please don't dismiss it as just garden-variety laziness. Seek professional help – they have the proper assessments to determine if it's clinical depression.

Of course, there's a vast spectrum between mild laziness and full-blown depressive disorders. You could be dealing with a moderate, somewhat impairing version somewhere in that middle ground that is still highly treatable through dedicated self-work. In these cases, developing better motivation habits and accountability systems, practising positive self-talk, optimising sleep, nutrition, exercise and purposefully designing your environment to enable productivity over slothfulness can go a long way.

The path ahead starts with radically attuning to your personal experiences without harsh judgment. Listen deeply to what is driving your motivational ebbs and flows with curiosity.

Be honest about whether it feels like an "I just need to get my act together" situation or if you are dealing with signs of dysfunction spiralling beyond conscious control. Seek help sooner than later if you are unsure which it is. If it's depression, honour that as the primary protocol through professional care plans, while exploring complementary lifestyle upgrades for recovery and prevention of future backslides.

Our human minds and psyches are vast and complex – rarely fitting neatly into binary categorizations. Our paths are highly personal dances between the shades of laziness and depression. No matter where you currently reside on that spectrum, the first step is meeting yourself with unconditional compassion and curiosity about what your soul is trying to communicate through these experiences. From there, the path forward keeps endlessly unfolding, one step after the next.

❑

The Habits That Stick

CHAPTER 5

Comfort Zone – Our Enemy

"Life always begins with one step outside of your comfort zone."

– Shannon L. Alder

You're lounging on your couch, binge-watching your favourite show and indulging in your favourite snacks. Everything feels perfect, right? No stress, no worries, just pure bliss in your self-imposed comfort zone. And you know what? There's nothing inherently wrong with having a comfort zone! We all need pockets of peace and predictability amidst the chaos of life. But what if you come to know that by staying in this zone, you are missing out on life's greatest adventures and opportunities?

The comfort zone is like a cosy blanket that lulls us into a false sense of contentment. However, at its core, it is really just a masterfully self-constructed prison cell to entrap our truest potential. And we stop growing, challenging ourselves or expanding our skills and perspectives. All sense of vitality, purpose and zest for life gradually erodes away.

This is why your comfort zone is ultimately one of the biggest pitfalls in overcoming laziness. It pacifies you with the false reassurance that treading water is perfectly acceptable. True lasting contentment and self-actualisation can only be found in continually seeking out new challenges that stretch and strengthen you over time.

Of course, leaving the comfort zone isn't exactly an alluring proposition for most of us. The human brain has an innate negativity bias that makes unknown risks, difficulties and failures feel far more impactful and threatening than the mere absence of positive opportunity.

Imagine yourself as an entrepreneur. You have built a dedicated following, secured lucrative brand deals and even launched your own successful venture. Life seems pretty sorted, right? You're living the dream, basking in the rewards of your perseverance and talent. But deep down, a nagging voice whispers, "Is this it? Is this the peak of your potential?" That once-burning passion that fuelled your hustle has started to simmer, and you can't shake the feeling that something is missing.

Sound familiar? We've all been there, haven't we? But the fact is advisable that the key to reigniting that fire within is to step into the unknown, embrace discomfort and challenge yourself in ways that stretch your limits.

Intellectually, we all know that routinely challenging ourselves is advisable and a good thing. That exponential growth and breakthroughs are born from uncomfortability. But taking that first step into uncharted territory feels like willingly jumping into a pit of snakes. This is precisely why the gravitational pull of the comfort zone is so powerfully addictive. It is quite literally the path of least resistance that our lazy, instinctual selves crave to default repeatedly.

Just think about how often you have resolved to break a bad habit or push past self-imposed limitations, only for the lure of your cosy familiar routine to suck you right back in. Or the number of potentially life-changing opportunities you have passed up out of a paralyzing fear of the unknown: that dream job that would require relocating, that unconventional relationship dynamic, that business idea demanding vulnerability and risk to pursue.

Let's take a moment to reflect on someone you admire, someone who has defied the odds and shattered barriers. Perhaps it's Ratan Tata, the visionary businessman who transformed the Tata Group into a global powerhouse. Or maybe it's Priyanka Chopra Jonas, the trailblazing actress and producer who conquered both Bollywood and Hollywood.

What sets these individuals apart from rest of the mediocre world? They refused to settle for the status quo. They boldly stepped out of their comfort zones time and time again, embracing risks and challenges that would have paralyzed most people with fear.

Of course, completely abandoning your comfort zone 24/7 is not exactly practical or sustainable either. An endless grind of chaotic hyper-productivity is a recipe for burnout, imbalanced living and irresponsible risks. The sweet spot emerges when you clearly notice old habits, fears, and limiting beliefs triggering the sudden urge to shrink back into that lethargic shell rather than embracing necessary discomfort. Those are the pivotal moments to pause and consciously make an active choice – do you want to stay rooted in the predictable smallness? Or muster the courage to keep evolving into the kicked-up-a-notch version of yourself again?

Once we connect deeply to the opportunity costs of perpetual stagnation, suddenly the temporary anxieties and uncertainties of growth start feeling far less intimidating. We become fuelled to make bigger waves in our lives again.

Start small by identifying one lower-risk area of your life to experiment with tiny nudges beyond your normal routine. Read a genre of book you would typically never explore. Take a different commute path and notice your new surroundings. Cook with a new-to-you cuisine or ingredient.

The goal is to build up your arousal zone tolerance so that embracing novel stresses and calculated risks doesn't feel so frightening or intimidating. Because at the end of the day, the lure of the comfort zone is rooted in fear. A deep, primal fear of leaving the known behind for new territory. Of risking embarrassment, failure, or having to exert more than the bare minimum effort.

So, lean into that discomfort, and you'll find freedom waiting on the other side. The freedom to evolve, self-actualize and experience all the richness that life has to offer instead of numbing stagnation.

❑

Chapter 6
Fear of Failure

"Failure is not the opposite of success; it's a part of success."

– Arianna Huffington

This quote hits home an uncomfortable reality that we all grapple with. Sure, we get that failing is inevitable when chasing meaningful goals and personal growth. But let's be honest – the fear of failure is still terrifying!

Fear of failure is a major driver behind laziness, constant procrastination and settling for less than our full potential. That nagging inner voice keeps warning us that making a concerted effort, taking risks and stepping out of our comfort zones is not worth the potential embarrassment of messing up.

So instead of fearlessly pursuing our biggest dreams, we instinctively play it safe. We retreat into our little bubbles, convincing ourselves is not better to avoid risking failure than to dare something extraordinary...and potentially fall short.

You know that feeling of endlessly delaying or making excuses to dodge challenging tasks or goals where you might fail? "I'll start that new business/go back to school/write that book tomorrow when I've got it all figured out perfectly." Sound familiar?

But beneath that surface-level procrastination lies a torrent of deep-rooted fears and catastrophic "what-if" scenarios about the implications of failure. Embarrassment, harsh criticism, wasted effort, feeling inadequate, or the belief that your self-worth hinges on achievements.

Most of us have been conditioned since childhood to avoid failure at all costs. As children, we saw the ridicule and mockery that followed striking out or missing a shot in games. We picked up on subtle messages from parents and teachers that not living up to expectations was a bad thing. So, even as adults, the prospect of failing at something important still sparks those primal fears of being rejected, ashamed, and cast out from the metaphorical "tribe." Our emotional brains don't always do logic – they just react based on those ingrained scripts.

This fear is what keeps so many of us stuck in neutral, always playing it small and safe to dodge any temporary embarrassments or setbacks. But here's the hard truth: Letting the fear of failure dictate your limits is a surefire way to undermine your greatest potential over time. It is a self-imposed prison trapping you in unsatisfying levels of unexpressed talent, all to avoid periodic discomforts.

At some point, you have to make a conscious choice. Do you want to keep coasting and playing things ultra-safe just to avoid the possibility of failure? Or are you prepared to start venturing boldly beyond what feels certain and comfortable, giving your biggest dreams a real shot?

Because failure is inevitable if you are aiming for anything meaningful or ambitious in life. It is simply part of the cyclical process of mastering new skills, mindsets, and accomplishing great things. The road is never straight and obstacle-free.

Learning to accept failure's inevitability – really internalizing that at your core – is so liberating. It means you don't have to waste precious energy avoiding or fearing it. Instead, you can focus that energy on developing resilience and finding lessons in your failures to apply going forward.

Think about it this way: What is truly worse – enduring temporary embarrassments or frustrations when you fall short of a goal? Or the haunting regret of never fully pursuing your dreams and deepest potential?

Because fear of failure often fuels a cycle of playing things way too small, squandering talents you were meant to develop and share with the world. It is self-doubt and laziness joining forces to convince you to underachieve.

Let's look at Oprah Winfrey as an inspiring example. The media mogul and philanthropist faced numerous failures and setbacks on her journey to success. She was fired from her first TV job as a news anchor and told she "wasn't fit for television."

But instead of letting that failure discourage her, Oprah used it as fuel. She refused to let someone else's limited perspective define her worth or potential. She persisted, honed her skills and eventually landed a gig hosting a low-rated talk show in Chicago.

It was through that opportunity that Oprah discovered her true calling and allowed her authenticity and empathy to shine through. The rest, as they say, is history. Oprah went on to build a multi-billion dollar media empire, become one of the most influential people in the world and inspire millions with her message of empowerment and resilience.

Oprah's ability to embrace failure as a part of the journey, rather than letting it derail her, is a testament to the power of perseverance and self-belief. She didn't let the fear of future failures hold her back from taking calculated risks and seizing opportunities.

The fear of failure often stems from a misguided belief that we must succeed at everything we attempt. But as Oprah's story shows, failure is an inevitable part of growth and success. It is how we respond to those failures that truly matters.

You can choose to let this be the day you break free from that self-sabotaging cycle and start welcoming failures as catalysts for building creativity, resilience and unstoppable drive in pursuing your highest self. Not feeling ashamed when you fall short, but getting radically curious about how to iterate and improve.

Surround yourself with examples of wildly successful people who turned past failures into their greatest training tools. People who openly shared how their biggest breakthroughs were forged through the very adversities they had the courage to grow from.

Remind yourself that without failure's refining fire to push through, we'd all stay hopelessly stunted and small versions of our potential selves. That fearing failure is really just fearing growth and fulfilment in disguise.

As that fear loosens its grip, watch as new reserves of motivation and stamina start flooding in. You will find yourself able to charge after ambitious targets while viewing any temporary growing pains as worthwhile investments in your evolution.

Most importantly, practise celebrating and finding success in simply daring to attempt bold pursuits – regardless of the outcome. Because wholeheartedly committing to risky endeavours is what makes you feel radically alive. That's where you unearth new aspects of your highest self.

So, embrace that perspective. Cultivate an appetite for failures, discomfort, and growing pains as the prices happily paid for admission into grander realms of fulfilment and self-actualization. Let the fear of failure motivate you into an audacious stance of perpetual becoming, not resignation.

What is the biggest failure of all? Playing it so safe and small that you leave your greatest music unshared, quietly fading away when you were destined for symphonic roars. Don't let fear be what diminishes the rare beauty of your human experience. Choose courage over complacency. It is the only way to live without regrets.

❑

CHAPTER 7

Perfectionism

"Perfectionism is a disease. Procrastination is a disease. Action is the cure."

– Richie Norton

The Illusion of Perfection

It sounds like a noble pursuit, doesn't it? Striving for flawlessness in everything we do. But what if you come to know that this seemingly virtuous trait could actually be holding you back, leading you down the path of laziness and inaction?

We often associate perfectionism with high achievers, those relentlessly pursuing excellence in their endeavours. But the reality is far more complex. Perfectionism is the constant need to be perfect in every aspect of life – work, relationships and personal goals. It is the unforgiving pursuit of flawlessness, setting impossibly high standards for oneself and others.

And herein lies the trap – perfectionism often leads to procrastination and avoidance of tasks. Let's explore this surprising connection.

The Paralysis of Perfectionism

Imagine you have a project to complete with a looming deadline. As a perfectionist, you want every detail to be flawless, every word perfect. But as you delve deeper into the task, you realise that achieving perfection is next to impossible.

So what do you do? You procrastinate

You delay starting the project because you fear that it will not meet your impossibly high standards. At the heart of perfectionism lies the fear of failure – 'the terror of making mistakes or falling short of expectations, both your own and others'.

This fear paralyses perfectionists, preventing them from taking action and getting things done. Instead of embracing imperfection as a natural part of the learning process, they see it as a sign of personal inadequacy.

The Cycle of Analysis Paralysis

Perfectionists have a tendency to overthink and overanalyse every decision they make. They get stuck in a cycle of *analysis paralysis*, unable to move forward till they have weighed every possible outcome. This leads to procrastination and indecision, further fuelling their laziness.

Perfectionists have an 'all-or-nothing mindset' – if they can't do something perfectly, they would rather not do it at all. This black-and-white thinking is detrimental to their productivity and can lead to chronic laziness. Instead of accepting incremental progress, they hold out for the unattainable perfect result.

The Pressure to Excel

Perfectionists often set unrealistic expectations for themselves, expecting nothing less than perfection in everything they do. This constant pressure to excel can be overwhelming, leading to burnout and mental exhaustion. As a result, they may avoid tasks altogether, preferring to retreat into the safety of inaction.

So, how do we break free from the perfectionist trap and overcome lassitude and laziness? The key lies in letting go of our need for perfection and embracing imperfection as a natural part of the human experience.

Strategies to Embrace Imperfection

1. **Set Realistic Goals:** Instead of aiming for perfection, set achievable goals that allow for mistakes and setbacks. Focus on progress rather than perfection.
2. **Practise Self-Compassion:** Be kind to yourself when you make mistakes or fall short of your expectations. Treat yourself with the same kindness and understanding that you would offer to a friend.
3. **Take Imperfect Action:** Instead of waiting for the perfect moment or the perfect conditions, take imperfect action and course-correct along the way. Action, even imperfect action, is better than inaction.
4. **Focus on the Process:** Shift your focus from the end result to the process itself. Enjoy the journey of learning and growth, rather than fixating on the destination.

5. **Celebrate Small Wins:** Recognise and celebrate even the smallest victories along the way. This will help you stay motivated and focused on the progress you are making, rather than getting bogged down by the pursuit of perfection.
6. **Surround Yourself with Supportive People:** Build a network of friends, family, and colleagues who understand and support your journey towards embracing imperfection. They can provide encouragement and perspective when you feel yourself slipping back into perfectionist or demanding tendencies.
7. **Practise Mindfulness:** Cultivate a mindfulness practise to help you stay grounded in the present moment and let go or give up the need for perfection. Mindfulness can help you become more accepting of imperfection and less judgmental of yourself and others.

The Path to Progress

Perfectionism may seem like a noble pursuit, but in reality, it often leads to procrastination and laziness. By letting go of our need for perfection and embracing imperfection, we can break free from the perfectionist trap and overcome laziness.

Remember, progress, not perfection, is the key to success. As Winston Churchill wisely said, "Perfection is the enemy of progress." So let go of perfection and start making progress today. Embrace the journey, celebrate your small wins, and trust that imperfection is not only inevitable but also a necessary part of growth and learning.

The path to progress is paved with imperfect steps, but each step moves you closer to your goals. So take that first imperfect step today, and watch as your momentum builds, carrying you towards the life you truly desire – a life free from the shackles of perfectionism and laziness.

❑

CHAPTER 8

Decision Paralysis

"The greatest power is often simple patience."

– E. Joseph Cossman

Have you ever found yourself stuck, unable to choose between two options or unsure which path to take? This phenomenon, known as **decision paralysis**, can be a major obstacle to productivity and a hidden cause of laziness. Let us explore this insidious state and learn how to overcome it.

The Paradox of Too Many Choices

Decision paralysis often strikes when we are overwhelmed by an abundance or plethora of choices. Whether it is deciding what to wear, what to eat, or which project to prioritize, having too many options can leave us feeling paralyzed and unable to take action.

In his book '*The Paradox of Choice*,' psychologist Barry Schwartz argues that having too many choices can actually decrease our satisfaction and happiness. When faced with an overwhelming number of options, we become anxious about making the wrong decision and fear missing out on better alternatives. As a result, we may procrastinate or avoid deciding altogether.

The Fear of Failure

At the heart of decision paralysis lies the fear of making mistakes. We worry that choosing the wrong option will lead to negative consequences or regret. This fear of failure immobilises us, preventing us from taking action and moving forward with our goals.

Steve Jobs, the late co-founder of Apple, was known for his ability to make tough decisions. In his words, "Deciding what not to do is as important as deciding what to do."

Analysis Paralysis: The Overthinking Trap

Analysis paralysis is a specific form of decision paralysis characterised by overthinking and overanalysing every possible outcome. We get bogged down in the details, endlessly weighing the pros and cons of each option without ever reaching a resolution. This excessive rumination drains our mental energy and leaves us feeling exhausted and demotivated.

Former US Secretary of State Colin Powell famously said, "Use the formula P=40 to 70, in which P stands for the probability of success and the numbers indicate the percentage of information acquired." This philosophy encourages making decisions with approximately 40-70 percent of the available information, rather than endlessly analysing every detail.

Decision Fatigue: The Mental Drain

Making decisions requires mental effort, and the more decisions we have to make, the more mentally fatigued we become. This phenomenon, known as decision fatigue, can impair our ability to make sound judgments and lead to poor or faulty decision-making. As our mental energy wanes, we become increasingly prone to laziness and procrastination.

Overcoming Decision Paralysis

So how do we break free from the grip of decision paralysis and reclaim our productivity? Here are some strategies to help you overcome decision paralysis and combat laziness:

1. **Limit Your Options:** Instead of overwhelming yourself with endless choices, narrow down your options to a manageable number. Focus on what truly matters and eliminate unnecessary alternatives.

2. **Set Priorities:** Identify your top priorities and allocate your time and energy accordingly. Focus on the tasks that will have the greatest impact and let go of less important decisions.

3. **Trust Your Instincts:** Learn to trust your gut instincts and make decisions based on intuition rather than over-analysis. Remember that there is rarely a "perfect" choice, and sometimes "good enough" is good enough.

4. **Break Tasks into Smaller Steps:** Break large decisions into smaller, more manageable steps and tackle them one at a time. This approach reduces overwhelm and makes it easier to take action.

5. **Embrace Imperfection:** Accept that mistakes are a natural part of the decision-making process, and that it's acceptable to make the occasional wrong choice. Focus on learning and growth rather than striving for perfection.

6. **Set Deadlines:** Impose self-imposed deadlines for making decisions. This creates a sense of urgency and prevents you from endlessly mulling over or considering options.

7. **Seek Advice:** Don't be afraid to seek advice from trusted friends, family members, or professionals. An outside perspective can often provide clarity and help you break through decision paralysis.

Decision paralysis can be a silent saboteur of productivity, leading to procrastination and laziness. By understanding the root causes of decision paralysis and implementing strategies to overcome it, we can break free from its grip and reclaim our ability to take decisive action.

Remember, as E. Joseph Cossman said, "The greatest power is often simple patience." So be patient with yourself, trust your instincts, and take decisive steps towards your goals. Embrace the journey, celebrate small wins, and let go of the need for perfection – because at the end of the day, progress, not perfection, is the key to success.

❑

Chapter 9

Parkinson's Law

"Work expands so as to fill the time available for its completion."

– C. Northcote Parkinson

Have you ever had an assignment or project with a pretty loose or flexible deadline, only to find yourself scrambling to get it done right at the last minute? Despite having or adequate ample time, the work still managed to expand and consume every bit of that runway.

If such situations sound familiar to your life, then you have experienced the bizarre effects of Parkinson's Law in full force. But don't worry; this *law* has nothing to do with any debilitating medical condition!

Coined in the 1950s by British historian and philosopher Cyril Northcote Parkinson, this principle simply observes how our tendency is for work to miraculously expand and fill whatever time window we allocate for it. Give yourself a year to finish something? It will absolutely take you a year. Only have a week? You'll somehow make it happen in that constraint.

Now you may be thinking...all right, so work expands to fill time – that is just human nature to procrastinate, right? While that's partially true, Parkinson's Law points to something much deeper at play. It is not simply our lazy tendency to put things off, but also very rational human behaviour around how we inherently budget and prioritise our efforts.

The core reason the law proves so pervasive is because of something called Student Syndrome – our brains' hardwiring to perform best under the pressure of deadlines. When we set vague, open-ended time bounds for a project, it doesn't light any motivational fire under us. But the second we impose a very real, consequential deadline, we become work machines!

In a sense, Parkinson's Law is just our brain's way of optimizing energy expenditure and resource usage. Why work at peak efficiency if there is no acute finish line or pressure? Your subconscious conserves effort till the deadline is imminent – only then does it unlocks that burst of concentrated focus required to execute.

Left unchecked, Parkinson's Law facilitates all sorts of debilitating time-sucks:

- Insane meeting proliferation and lack of schedule control
- Endless revisions and revisiting work rather than shipping
- Overcomplicating every project and task with unnecessary steps

- Drowning in process and admin instead of action
- Perpetual procrastination and avoidance when no hard deadlines loom or appear

Sound miserable? It absolutely can be, if you let Parkinson's Law run roughshod over your days. The antidote is injecting imposed constraints and restrictions on your time. As counterintuitive as it sounds, putting stricter time bounds and deadlines on yourself is the most efficient way to supercharge your output.

Think about the times in your own life when you have felt "in the zone" and your productivity was off the charts – can you pinpoint what was different? Likely those instances came when you had to work within very clear, rigid timelines that left no wiggle room. Your energy, focus, and execution all ratcheted up accordingly.

Utilising Parkinson's Law – and imposing time-boxes rather than letting work expand infinitely – is a core tenet of methodologies like Scrum, Getting Things Done, the Pomodoro Technique, and others. But you don't need any formal framework to harness the power of time constraints. Just start setting ruthless deadlines to create pressure and urgency that keeps your work output under control.

Powerful Ways to Leverage Time Bounds

- **Set "Closing Time" for Projects and Tasks:** Everything gets a hard stop or finish line beyond which you are done. For projects, scope it out in phases. Phase 1 must ship by Date X – no exceptions. For recurring tasks, set a time limit (ex: capping weekly reporting at 60 min max no matter what). When the clock strikes "closing time", you are done.

- **Use Countdown Timers/Reminders:** A big reason work expands is the lack of perceived immediacy. But set a countdown app or calendar alerts leading up to your deadlines, and you'll definitely feel that escalating pressure! Reign in scope creep with constant reminders of closing time approaching.
- **Time-Box Your Calendar:** Divide your day into "work boxing" sessions – time blocks dedicated to exclusively focused bursts on high priorities. You are not allowed to do anything else during those windows before moving to the next time-box. This quarantines Parkinson bloat and ensures you actually finish what you start.
- **Batch Low-Priority Activities:** Stop letting inconsequential maintenance tasks dominate your day. Batch them into a single contained window like "Email/ Admin Day" every two weeks. Apply harsh time bounds on those peripheral activities so they don't gradually expand into daily distractions that derail priorities.
- **Create Artificial Constraints:** For nebulous open-ended projects, impose your own arbitrary deadline or time limit to instil the deadline pressure. For example: "I'm allocating no more than three weeks to Phase 1 of this project." You would be amazed how much more focused you work when false constraints are in play.

Ultimately, you need to make Parkinson's Law work for you rather than against your productivity. Don't just let responsibilities expand into whatever spare room exists in your calendar and attention! Instead, use deadlines proactively and frequently to maintain momentum.

It may feel somewhat counterintuitive to consciously restrict your time on tasks. But that pressure will keep you focused and working with efficient intensity rather than lackadaisically letting projects bleed into perpetuity. You will be shipping higher volumes of quality work in the same stretch as a result.

A famous example of Parkinson's effects: in the 1960s, a sharpened focus on sending people to the moon necessitated compressing delivery times for insanely complex engineering projects that would normally take a decade. But by instilling extremely rigid deadlines of just a few years, researchers buckled down and worked with maniacal focus to accomplish those gravity-defying missions on the accelerated timeline.

So no more lazily spacing things out and letting dreadful scope creep reign! Whether for personal tasks, business projects, or even overarching life goals, create those unyielding constraints and delivery dates to light some urgency under yourself.

Harnessing Parkinson's Law won't be comfortable at first. You will feel immense pressure as deadlines loom and nerves jangle about whether you can actually finish everything in time. But that's good mental resistance training! Over time, that compressed energy only heightens your abilities to work intensely, prioritise relentlessly, and deliver high-quality results right on schedule.

Of course, balance matters here too – you don't want to careen into burnout by imposing ridiculous delivery windows and perpetual crunch time. Give yourself enough breathing room to maintain steady focus, but not so much open space that motivation dissipates into procrastination.

But whether in bite-sized chunks or overarching goal time-boxes, regularly imposing those limits allows you to "spend" your time more consciously and intentionally. No more watching the days bleed away only to find important work still lingering amid poor execution.

Parkinson's Law is the perfect forcing function to supercharge productivity, destroy procrastination habits and start living by design rather than default. Use it wisely and you will be amazed at what you can cram or fit into each day.

❑

Mindful Practices

CHAPTER 10

Enabling Growth

"The only way to do great work is to love what you do. If you haven't found it yet, keep looking. Don't settle."

— Steve Jobs

In our journey to overcome laziness or inertia and cultivate a more productive lifestyle, one of the most powerful tools at our disposal is the practise of embracing growth. This concept, rooted in psychologist Carol Dweck's research on mindset, revolves around the idea that our beliefs about our abilities profoundly influence our behaviour and success. In this chapter, we will explore how adopting a growth mindset can transform our approach to challenges, setbacks and personal development.

Psychologist Carol Dweck's studies have identified two primary mindsets: *the fixed mindset and the growth mindset.* Individuals with a fixed mindset believe that their abilities and talents are innate and unchangeable. They view challenges as threats to their self-esteem and are more likely to give up in the face of obstacles or impediments. In contrast, those with a growth mindset see challenges as opportunities for growth and learning. They believe that through effort and perseverance, they can improve their skills and abilities over time.

Embracing a growth mindset empowers us to approach life with a sense of optimism and resilience. Instead of viewing setbacks as failures, we see them as valuable learning experiences that contribute to our personal and professional growth. This shift in perspective allows us to bounce back from adversity stronger and more determined than ever before.

Developing a growth mindset is not something that happens overnight; it requires deliberate effort and practise. Here are some strategies to help you cultivate a growth mindset and harness its transformative power:

1. **Embrace Challenges:** Instead of avoiding challenges, seek them out as opportunities for growth and self-improvement. Embrace the discomfort that comes with stepping outside of your comfort zone, knowing that it is essential for personal growth.

2. **Learn from Failure:** Rather than viewing failure as a reflection of your abilities, see it as a stepping stone on the path to success. Take the time to reflect on what went wrong, extract valuable lessons from the experience, and use them to inform your future actions.

3. **Cultivate Resilience:** Develop resilience by adopting a positive attitude and persevering in the face of adversity. Understand that setbacks are temporary and that you have the strength and determination to overcome or surmount them.

4. **Seek Feedback:** Be open to feedback and constructive criticism, as they provide valuable insights into areas where you can improve. Instead of taking feedback personally, view it as an opportunity to learn and grow.

5. **Set Meaningful Goals:** Set ambitious yet achievable goals that inspire and motivate you to push beyond your limits. Break them down into smaller, manageable steps and celebrate your progress along the way.

Now that we understand the principles of growth mindset, let's explore how we can apply them to our daily lives:

- **In the Workplace:** Approach challenges at work with a growth or progressive mindset, viewing them as opportunities to develop new skills and expand your capabilities. Seek out feedback from colleagues and supervisors to continually improve and grow professionally.
- **In Relationships:** Adopt a growth mindset in your relationships, recognizing that they require effort and commitment to thrive. Be open to feedback from your partner and willing to work through challenges together, knowing that growth and learning are essential for a healthy relationship.
- **In Personal Development:** Embrace a growth mindset in your personal development journey, setting ambitious goals and taking deliberate steps to achieve them. Celebrate your progress along the way and use setbacks as opportunities to learn and grow stronger.

Embracing growth is not just about achieving success; it is about cultivating a mindset that allows us to thrive in the face of adversity and uncertainty. By adopting a growth mindset, we can overcome laziness, push past our limitations, and achieve our full potential. So keep striving for growth, keep pushing yourself to new heights and never settle for anything less than your best.

❑

CHAPTER 11

Self-Compassion

"Self-compassion is simply giving the same kindness to ourselves that we would give to others."

– Christopher Germer

We have all been there – stuck in a vicious cycle of self-criticism and negative self-talk, leading to procrastination and a feeling of laziness. But what if there was a way to break free from this trap? Enter self-compassion, a powerful tool that can transform our lives and help us overcome laziness.

What is Self-Compassion?

Self-compassion is all about treating ourselves with the same kindness, understanding and forgiveness that we would offer to a dear friend. It is about embracing our imperfections and recognising that we deserve love and acceptance, just as we are.

According to psychologist Kristin Neff, self-compassion consists of three key components:

1. **Self-Kindness:** Being gentle and understanding with ourselves during times of pain or failure, rather than harshly judging or criticising ourselves.

2. **Common Humanity**: Recognising *that* suffering and imperfection are universal experiences shared by all human beings, rather than feeling isolated or alone in our struggles.

3. **Mindfulness:** Approaching our thoughts and emotions with a balanced perspective, acknowledging them without becoming overwhelmed by them.

Benefits of Self-Compassion

Embracing self-compassion can have a profound impact on our mental and emotional well-being, as well as our daily productivity:

- **Reduced Stress and Anxiety:** By soothing our inner critics and providing ourselves with emotional support, self-compassion helps to lower levels of stress and anxiety.

- **Increased Resilience:** Self-compassionate individuals are better able to bounce back from setbacks and adversity, as they approach challenges with kindness and understanding.

- **Improved Productivity:** Self-compassion can enhance your performance, creativity and innovation by fostering a positive and supportive mindset.

- **Greater Emotional Regulation:** Self-compassionate individuals are better equipped to manage difficult emotions and cope with negative experiences, as they are less likely to engage in self-destructive behaviours or ruminate on their problems.

J.K. Rowling, the acclaimed author of the Harry Potter series, is a prime example of the power of self-compassion. Despite facing numerous rejections and personal hardships, Rowling persevered and eventually achieved remarkable success. In her 2008 Harvard Commencement speech, she emphasised the importance of embracing failure and being kind to oneself, stating, "It is impossible to live without failing at something, unless you live so cautiously that you might as well not have lived at all – in which case, you fail by default."

Cultivating Self-Compassion

Self-compassion is a skill that can be learned and practised. Here are some practical tips to get you started:

1. **Acknowledge and Validate Your Feelings:** Remind yourself that your feelings and experiences are valid, and that you are not alone in your struggles. Recognize the common humanity in your challenges.

2. **Practise Mindfulness:** Be mindful of your thoughts and emotions, but don't let negative or irrational thoughts control or define you. Replace them with positive, realistic, and constructive thoughts.

3. **Appreciate Your Uniqueness:** Remember that you are part of a larger community of people who share your struggles, challenges, and aspirations. However, also appreciate your uniqueness and diversity, without comparing yourself to others or idealising them.

4. **Follow the Self-Compassion Checklist:**
   - Am I being kind and understanding towards myself?
   - Do I acknowledge my shortcomings and failures as experiences rather than defining traits?
   - Am I keeping my negative feelings in perspective and not letting them overwhelm me?

Overcoming Obstacles to Self-Compassion

Practising self-compassion may not always feel easy or comfortable. You might face internal resistance, guilt, or fear, worrying that self-compassion will make you "soft" or "lazy." You might also encounter external obstacles, such as societal norms or expectations that promote self-criticism over self-kindness.

However, it is essential to be patient, persistent and flexible with yourself on this journey. Don't expect perfection or instant results, and don't judge yourself for struggling or slipping up. Instead, find your own pace, style, and methods that work for you. Experiment with different techniques and seek support from others who value and practise self-compassion.

Oprah Winfrey, the renowned media mogul and philanthropist, has been an advocate for self-compassion and personal growth. In an interview with Brené Brown, she shared her perspective on self-acceptance: "The greatest gift you can give yourself is the gift of self-acceptance. It is the key to living a life filled with peace, joy and contentment."

Self-compassion is not just a fluffy or vague concept; it is a powerful tool for transformation and personal growth. By treating ourselves with kindness, understanding, and acceptance, we can break free from the cycle of self-criticism and embrace our true selves.

As the wise words of Christopher Germer remind us, "Self-compassion is simply giving the same kindness to ourselves that we would give to others." So, be kind to yourself, embrace your humanity, and watch as self-compassion becomes the fuel that propels you forward on your journey to a more fulfilling life, free from the shackles of laziness.

❑

Chapter 12

Motivation

"Motivation is the catalyzing ingredient for every successful innovation."

– Clayton Christensen

Motivation is the driving force that propels us to take action and accomplish our goals. It is the fuel that keeps us moving forward, even when faced with challenges and setbacks. In the context of overcoming laziness or inertia and fostering productivity, motivation plays a crucial role as a mindful practise.

Imagine motivation as a powerful engine that can propel you out of the quicksand of procrastination and inertia. It is the spark that ignites your passion, focus, and determination, transforming mere intentions into tangible results. Without motivation, even the most well-laid plans and resolutions can fall flat, leaving us stuck in a cycle of unfulfilled potential.

The beauty of motivation lies in its ability to transcend external circumstances. While external factors like rewards, deadlines, or peer pressure can provide temporary boosts, true motivation stems from within – a deep-rooted desire to grow, achieve, and contribute something meaningful to the world.

At its core, motivation is deeply intertwined with our values, beliefs, and aspirations. It is the driving force that compels us to pursue our dreams, overcome obstacles, and push beyond our self-imposed limitations. When we tap into our intrinsic motivations, we unlock a well-spring of energy and commitment that can sustain us through even the most daunting challenges.

One powerful aspect of motivation is its ability to shape our mindset. When we are genuinely motivated, we approach tasks and goals with a positive, solution-oriented attitude. We become more resilient, adaptable, and open to learning from setbacks. Motivation fuels our creativity, allowing us to explore innovative approaches and embrace calculated risks.

In the realm of goal setting, motivation plays a pivotal role. It is the bridge that connects our aspirations to tangible action steps. By setting clear, meaningful goals that align with our values and passions, we create a powerful motivational anchor that keeps us focused and driven.

External motivators, such as rewards, recognition, or competition, can provide valuable short-term boosts, but true, lasting motivation often comes from within. When we cultivate a sense of purpose, personal growth, and self-mastery, we tap into an inexhaustible well of motivation that transcends fleeting external incentives.

Cultivating motivation as a mindful practise involves several key elements:

1. **Self-Awareness:** Understand your values, strengths and intrinsic drivers. Reflect on what truly inspires and energises you and align your goals accordingly.

2. **Positive Self-Talk:** Reframe negative self-talk and limiting beliefs that undermine your motivation. Celebrate small wins and practise self-compassion when faced with setbacks.

3. **Visualisation:** Engage in regular visualisation exercises, vividly imagining the successful achievement of your goals. This mental rehearsal can prime or prepare your mind for action and reinforce your motivation.

4. **Accountability:** Surround yourself with supportive individuals or join communities that share your goals and aspirations. Accountability partners can provide encouragement, feedback and a sense of shared commitment.

5. **Habit Formation:** Break down larger goals into manageable, actionable steps and integrate them into your daily routine. Consistency breeds momentum and momentum fuels motivation.

6. **Mindfulness:** Practise mindfulness techniques, such as meditation or deep breathing exercises, to cultivate present-moment awareness and reduce the distractions that can undermine your motivation.

Remember, motivation is a renewable resource. Like a muscle, it requires regular exercise and nourishment. By embracing motivation as a mindful practise, you can tap into an endless well-spring of energy, focus and determination, propelling you towards the realisation of your dreams and aspirations.

In the journey to overcome laziness and embrace productivity, motivation is your personal compass, guiding you through the challenges and obstacles that inevitably arise. Embrace it, nurture it and let it be the driving force that transforms your intentions into tangible results, one mindful step at a time.

❑

CHAPTER 13

Discipline

"With self-discipline most anything is possible."

– Theodore Roosevelt

Discipline is the secret sauce that separates the dreamers from the doers. It is that inner drill sergeant that whips you into shape and keeps you marching toward your goals. If motivation is the initial spark to get you fired up or enthusiastic, discipline is the long-burning fuel that keeps that fire raging.

Without discipline, even your grandest plans and ambitions are merely wishful thinking. They remain trapped in the cosy prison of laziness and procrastination. But with discipline installed as a mindful practise, you develop the persevering habits and routines to turn your fleeting intentions into tangible results.

Picture discipline as an internal suit of armour fortifying you against distractions, setbacks and that snooze button's siren call. It is the reinforced scaffolding that prevents you from plunging back into the quicksand of inertia after every false start and stumble.

At its core, discipline is about developing systems and lifestyles of productive habits. These sustainable routines become ingrained so that showing up and taking consistent action towards your goals is the default rather than something you have to muster up daily.

It is about commanding and directing your most precious resources – your time, energy, focus and environment – with military precision toward your highest priorities. With discipline, there is no more diffusing those finite reserves across trivial distractions and busywork. You become a SEAL-level executor laser-focused on the vital tasks that actually move your important needles.

There are several key dimensions to discipline that interlock to amplify your productivity and personal effectiveness:

1. **Time Mastery:** You can't expect to conquer laziness till you first gain control of your calendar and schedule. Disciplined time management involves:
    - Conducting audits to identify productivity leaks
    - Time-boxing dedicated work periods on your calendar
    - Defending those precious focus windows like a navy seal
    - Mastering the ballet of batching similar tasks
2. **Habit Development:** Routines and habits are discipline's greatest force-multipliers. When vital

patterns like exercise, nutrition, sleep and more become second nature:

- You'll maintain them automatically with minimal friction
- Keystone habits pave the way for discipline's ripple effect
- You conserve mental energy for your highest priorities

3. **Environment Design:** You are forever reverting to the easiest surrounding option. By designing disciplined environments, you:
   - Reduce unavoidable distractions and detours
   - Install obvious cues that trigger desired actions
   - Leverage public accountability to stay committed
4. **Prioritisation:** Not all tasks are created equal. Disciplined prioritizing ensures you never mistake busyness for effectiveness. Key practises include:
   - Focusing relentlessly on your highest-leverage activities
   - Filtering out the trivial peripheral busywork and time-wasters
   - Batching and eliminating lower-impact tasks
5. **Resilience:** Perfection is unrealistic and discipline's worst enemy. Building resilience allows you to:

- Maintain consistency through inevitable failure periods
- Celebrate small wins to nurture lasting motivation
- View setbacks as data to refine your approach

6. **Mindfulness:** At its core, discipline stems from heightened self-awareness. Mindfulness practises like meditation:
    - Embed you in the present to override distractions
    - Build pattern-interrupt abilities for poor unproductive habits
    - Foster self-compassion during the growth process

When skilfully integrated, these various disciplines create a robust operating system for your life's biggest goals and ambitions. Just think about having your very own internal drill sergeant barking:

"Did that just move you forward or was it worthless busywork? No slacking, back to your highest priorities!"

With that sentinel of discipline providing the framework, your time, energy and life regain their purposefulness and trajectory. Every waking moment is maximized for continual progress towards your biggest visions.

While motivation's flames may flicker, true discipline provides the steady unshakable hand steering you forward. It is the empowering foundation that allows other pivotal mindfulness practises like gratitude, acceptance and resilience to thrive.

The true beauty of discipline lies in its compounding effect over time. Every disciplined choice erects another brick in the great wall separating you from laziness. As those micro-decisions accumulate into ingrained routines, what was once a struggle becomes automatic.

Imagine finally outgrowing the exhausting resistance to "mustering motivation" every morning. With discipline, your pre-programmed productive routines fire off or proceed like clockwork at your first trigger – no exhausting mental negotiations required. You just listen and follow the drill sergeant's lead.

This is how big dreams proceed from imagination to manifestation. This is how simple habits like making your bed spawn ripple effects across your entire day and life's trajectory. With discipline installed as a mindful operating system, you code your days for continual progress, productivity and purpose.

In the war on laziness, motivation is an inspiring battle cry, but discipline is the elite training regimen to win the campaign. It is the mindful practise that develops the unwavering habits and conditioning to sustain victory long-term. No more spinning your wheels or backsliding into old patterns. With discipline cultivated, you gain the power to author your life's script in alignment with your highest ideals.

❑

CHAPTER 14

Outcomes

"He who fears being conquered is sure of defeat."

–Napoleon Bonaparte

Outcome is the guiding light that serves as your compass in the battle against laziness. Without a clear vision of the outcome you desire, your efforts will scatter like a rudderless ship adrift on open seas. Committing to an outcome with unwavering focus is a pivotal mindful practise.

Think of your ideal outcome like a blazing beacon calling you home from the hazy fog of aimlessness and procrastination. It provides both inspiration to propel you forward and a tangible target to orient all your energies. An outcome firmly locked into your mind's eye becomes a self-fulfilling prophecy.

Defining and visualizing a compelling outcome awakens the forces of desire and necessity within you. Desire stokes the internal fire and hunger to make it happen, while necessity summons relentless resourcefulness to find a way. With a clear outcome illuminated, you'll always have abundance of both motivation, determination and grit coursing through your veins.

Dimensions of Outcome

1. **Clarity:** A vague or ambiguous outcome provides no guiding light. It lacks the emotional resonance and pragmatic details to activate your determination. Craft an outcome vision that is:
    - Specific and granular in its description
    - Multi-sensory and vividly imagined
    - Rooted in your core values and aspirations
2. **Compelling:** For an outcome to inspire tireless energy and effort, it must be one that quite literally compels you from the depths. Design an outcome that is:
    - Intrinsically motivating on a profound level
    - Exciting and aligned with your greater purpose
    - Stretching your limits while remaining achievable
3. **Projected:** While the present moment is pivotal, your mind's greatest power is the ability to vividly project and pre-live outcomes in advance. Learn to:
    - Frequently visualize and emotionalize the outcome achieved
    - Embed positive future memories of pride and fulfilment
    - Develop an unwavering steadfast subjective faith in its realization
4. **Adaptability:** Rigid attachment to a singular outcome invites frustration and surrender when obstacles arise. Adopt an outlook that is:

- Committed to an general direction while flexible on paths
- Willing to course-correct and pivot your approach
- Resilient in the face of challenges and setbacks

While we cannot directly control outcomes themselves, mastering this mindful practise grants you authorship over your state and actions from which they arise. With your dream outcome illuminated:

- Your priorities become clear and distractions fade
- You cultivate the hunger and tenacity to handle any roadblock
- Self-discipline and consistency start compounding automatically
- You develop a potent third driving force of inspired necessity

Consider your personal Mount Everest, that long-standing ambition or "white whale" that's always seemed impossibly out of reach. It could be a successful business, accomplished work of art or even just optimising your life and well-being.

For most, this dream sits marooned in the dreaded "Someday Isle" – something they'll get to eventually after first conquering a litany of other obstacles. But by using your ideal outcome itself as a motivating force and guiding star, you steer your ship full steam ahead towards those uncharted waters rather than anchoring indefinitely in procrastination's safe harbour.

With a razor-sharp outcome vision at your holistic level, you begin making pivotal micro-choices and routine optimisations with that destiny in mind. Rather than cycle through the usual distractions and indulgences, you start saying "no" to whatever does not serve your ultimate "yes." An empowered life of discipline and intentionality begins emerging automatically.

The journey will never unfold perfectly, but cultivating this mindful practise ensures you always get back on track with learned course corrections. When unexpected storms of chaos and challenges arise, your guiding outcome beacon pierces the darkness to realign your trajectory.

In this way, your grandest **one day** outcomes don't wait for all the planets to perfectly align first. They begin victoriously unfolding today within the context of your imperfect present circumstances.

Just as a captain can chart a ship's heading solely with outcome coordinates in mind, an intended outcome singularity can attune and direct the full power of your focus, intention and actions – regardless of prevailing winds or conditions.

Of course, arriving at a genuinely compelling outcome vision itself requires going deep within. You must get radiantly and absolutely honest with yourself about what you truly want from your finite life force. What dreams lie buried under surface layers of distraction and resignation? What ambitions lie waiting to be liberated from limiting beliefs or perceived obstacles?

Productive exercise and journaling can provide portals to access your unconscious aspirations. Additionally, studying the lives and outcomes of mentors and role models can spark inspiration for previously unimagined possibilities. What outcomes are they embodying that perhaps you'd like to experience yourself?

With sustained self-discovery and imagination, an exciting outcome inevitably crystallizes out of the ether – one that stirs your soul, thrills your ambition, and imbues you with an internal locus of control and possibility.

Once locked into this compelling vision, the work of manifesting it into physical reality becomes almost secondary. The outcome itself already shifts your psychology into an empowered creative state oriented fully around making it so.

This mindful practise becomes an activating force propelling you into a more disciplined, elevated experiential plane. Obstacles are embraced as interim path-renderers rather than momentum-killers. Each step navigated with outcome certainty provides sustaining fulfilment in and of itself. Aligned being and action become one harmonious flow experience.

In the perennial fight against inertia and resignation, few mindful practises are as potent or transformative as committing to a definitive desired outcome. It is the activating force that alchemizes your latent ambitions into reality, while simultaneously blessing you with the determination and resourcefulness required to navigate any interim terrain.

With a clear and compelling outcome illuminating your path, motivation becomes automatic, procrastination absurd, and challenges accepted as rendered stepping stones in their proper context – not permanent roadblocks to be feared or surrendered to.

An outcome firmly rooted within you as a guiding force cannot be derailed or extinguished until it's realized in the physical world as intended. In this way, your dream's destiny is sealed once its vibrant vision is seared into your consciousness. Everything then becomes simply a matter of walking the path it reveals and celebrating the fulfilling journey itself.

❑

CHAPTER 15

Objectivity

"The highest form of self-respect is to admit our errors and mistakes and make amends for them."

– Confucius

We all have blind spots and biases that can sabotage our efforts to kick laziness to the curb. Our minds are experts at spinning tales and making up or inventing convenient excuses to stay in our safe, cosy, lazy status quo. However, objectivity acts as a powerful tool to cut through this mental clutter and see reality for what it is.

Truth and objectivity ultimately prove the strongest forces to overpower the ego's lazy inertia. When you can no longer hide behind stories and fictions, what is left is the powerful objectivity to accept full responsibility for your life's direction. In this space, laziness loses its seduction once uncloaked by raw reality. And your highest vision and purpose are empowered to become viscerally realized.

What is Objectivity?

Objectivity is the practise of stepping outside your subjective bubble to gain a clear, impartial perspective. It is about separating fact from fiction in your mind and dismantling the mental prisons and labyrinths we manufacture to stay trapped in our comfort zones.

The Power of Objectivity

Only from a place of radical objectivity can you accurately identify what is holding you back, design effective solutions, and forge an honest way forward. It provides a crucial 30,000-foot overview to witness yourself with cleansing detachment.

Ray Dalio, the billionaire founder of Bridgewater Associates, is a strong proponent of objectivity. In his book *Principles*, he emphasizes the importance of radical truth-seeking and challenging one's own beliefs. He encourages his employees to be brutally honest with him, even if it means pointing out his mistakes or flaws.

Principles of Objectivity

To master objectivity as a mindful practise, there are several powerful principles to integrate:

1. **Separating Facts from Stories:** Examine the current situation circumstances devoid of editorializing, factual causes and conditions, and personal responsibility.
2. **Killing Your Darlings:** Identify your "sacred cows" that may be holding you back, and let go or give up unhelpful ways with courage and self-love.
3. **Operating in A or B:** Observe current circumstances with lucid neutrality, run hypotheticals from a place

of curiosity, and make unemotional course corrections based on what is working or not.

4. **Widening Your View:** Actively seek out differing expert and peer perspectives, look at situations through a higher "altitude" lens, and identify potential blindspots or biases.
5. **Inner Self-Honesty:** Become radically honest with yourself about your truths, let go of stories or pretences projected for others, and operate from a place of brutal self-accountability.

Oprah Winfrey, the celebrated media mogul, has often spoken about the importance of objectivity and self-awareness. In an interview, she shared, "The biggest adventure you can take is to live the life of your dreams. But you have to be honest with yourself first. You have to take an objective dispassionate look at your life and make the necessary changes to move forward."

Overcoming Obstacles to Objectivity

Stepping outside our subjective selves to gain objectivity is anything but easy or natural. Our egos loathe questioning our cosy familiar beliefs and conditioned response patterns. Rising above those mental protectors and operating in openness and curiosity requires tremendous mindfulness.

Practises for Cultivating Objectivity

There are powerful practises to cultivate a mindset of objectivity, such as:

- Thought-clearing meditations to disengage from mental narratives
- Regularly soliciting feedback from those with alternate perspectives
- Journaling or personal inventories to interrogate your honest truths
- Adopting a "Beginner's Mind" mentality to see with fresh eyes
- Pushing yourself into new experiences to reveal hidden assumptions

Embracing Radical Objectivity

Fundamentally, objectivity requires seeing your ego as something to accept and observe rather than be controlled by. It means shifting or moving from subjective self-narratives of limitation to an objective stance of openness, accountability, and empowered responsibility.

Once installed, objectivity provides radical dispassionate clarity to see why your current strategies or behaviours may be underperforming. It allows you to transcend the mental loops and limiting beliefs so you can make authentic adjustments for accelerated results.

In the fight against laziness, the ultimate enemy is often... you. Or more accurately, the fictional stories, avoidance patterns and subjective blinders your psyche has constructed. Objectivity acts as the mighty mindful warrior to slay the dragons of self-deception.

With radical objectivity as your integrated lens, unproductive patterns become laid bare rather than perpetually rationalized. Unacknowledged limiting beliefs get revealed and dissolved. Laziness becomes absolutely untenable once stripped of its cosy complacent fictional disguises.

Truth and objectivity ultimately prove the strongest forces to overpower the ego's lazy inertia. When you can no longer hide behind stories and fictions, what is left is the powerful objectivity to accept full responsibility for your life's direction. In this space, laziness loses its seduction once uncloaked by raw reality, and your highest vision and purpose are empowered to become viscerally realised.

❑

Healthy Practices

CHAPTER 16

You Are What You Eat

"Let food be thy medicine and medicine be thy food."

– Hippocrates

You've heard the phrase "you are what you eat" – but have you truly internalised just how profound those words are? The foods you put into your body quite literally shape your energy levels, cognitive abilities, emotional state and physical vitality from the inside out.

Think of your dietary intake as the raw building materials constructing your body's biochemistry and operating system in real-time. When you consume low-quality, nutrient-depleted ingredient sources, you are essentially running your life on corrupted code and subpar fuel. Is it any wonder feelings of fatigue, brain fog, irritability and sloth so often follow?

In this ultra-processed, industrialised age of faux-foods, treating your dietary intake as a conscious healthy practise is absolutely paramount. We are constantly bombarded with culinary misinformation combined with cheap, hyper-palatable calorie sources engineered to short-circuit our rational decision making.

Today's food environment ensures putting in minimal thought or effort results in a highly catabolic diet wreaking inflammatory havoc on your system. That is why adopting an intentional, back-to-basics approach for what you put in your body has become so vitally important.

On a deep functional level, your dietary (intake impacts critical pathways including):

- **Energy Production:** The foods you eat literally build new cells while providing the raw materials to optimally generate ATP energy for fuelling physical and mental activities. High-quality proteins, healthy fats, nutrients and phytonutrients enable maximum vigour.
- **Cognitive Function:** Your brain's neurological processes are 100 percent dependent on receiving ample levels of various vitamins, minerals, antioxidants and nourishing fats. Nutrient deficiencies can directly hamper focus, memory, emotional regulation and more.
- **Hormone Regulation:** Vitamin and mineral cofactors control your body's endocrine system production of hormones like testosterone, estrogen, insulin, thyroid, cortisol and more. Imbalances can throw your entire system out of control.
- **Gut Health:** With 70 percent + of your immune system situated in your gut, microbiome balance is paramount. An over-processed diet destroys beneficial bacteria and causes inflammation that extends far beyond just digestive issues.

When you eat a suboptimal diet of empty calorie sources, you are effectively asphyxiating your cellular regenerative processes and starving your body of what it craves most. Is it any wonder fatigue,brainfog and listlessness tend to follow?

But beyond just avoidance of detrimental health impacts, premium fuel also optimizes your human biological software to operate at its absolute highest level. With clean whole foods providing an abundance of energizing nourishment:

- Neurotransmitters like dopamine and serotonin amplify motivation and positive mindset.
- Carbohydrate-dense foods enable laser focus and productive "flow" periods.
- Proteins and micronutrients accelerate muscle recovery and tissue repair.
- Anti-inflammatory benefits enhance mood, focus and overall zest for life.
- Simply expressed, you move from idling in a perpetual unsatisfying slog to performing as the naturally vibrant, effective and inspired human being you were designed to be.
- So what are the core tenets of eating for cognitive and metabolic optimization as a healthy practise?

Anti-Inflammatory Focus

The standard American diet consisting of highly-processed foods, refined ingredients and industrial seed oils is the #1 driver of systemic inflammation and metabolic disarray.

- Focus on getting ample antioxidants, fiber and anti-inflammatory nutrient sources like leafy greens, berries, fatty fish, turmeric.
- Reduce or eliminate processed seed/vegetable oils which are loaded with oxidized pro-inflammatory fats.
- Cycle in periods of lower carbohydrate/sugar intake to allow systemic inflammation levels to resettle.

Maximise Micronutrient Density

Modern foods are increasingly nutrient-depleted in terms of the essential vitamins, minerals and phytonutrients your body craves for optimal regeneration and regulation.

- Consume plenty of nutrient-dense whole foods like organ meats, seafood, eggs, cruciferous vegetables.
- Consider supplementing bioavailable forms of nutrients you may be commonly deficient in like magnesium, vitamin D, zinc, etc.
- Focus on getting ample servings of probiotic foods to promote gut microbiome flourishing.

Healthy Fat Prioritisation

For too long we have been inundated with misguided “low-fat” advice that’s been disastrous for public health. Your body and brain require ample levels of healthy fats to thrive.

- Focus on sources like fatty fish, olive oil, avocados, nuts and seeds for balancing your omega fatty acids.

- Consume plenty of fat-soluble vitamins which require sufficient dietary fat for absorption
- Low-fat often equals low-satiety leading to overeating – fats increase satiety signalling

Strategic Carb Cycling

While carbohydrate sources are vital for energy and cognitive function, hitting reset periods with lower intakes can be highly therapeutic.

- Pursue lower-carb periods to increase fat-burning metabolism and reduce inflammation
- But then cycle back up around more demanding training sessions or for productivity
- Focus on slow-digesting complex carbs like vegetables, berries, root starches and whole grains

Intuitive Eating for Awareness

Unfortunately most have lost touch with their body's innate hunger/satiety signaling system and context for portions.

- Eat when hungry, stop when full – disconnect from rigid food rules or plans.
- Check-in before, during and after meals to note how different foods make you feel.
- Give your body time to register satiety by slowing down and removing distractions.

Hydration Prioritisation

Water accounts for 60-70 percent of your body's composition and is essential for cellular communication and overall systemic function.

- Monitor urine colour and drink sufficient amounts of clean, filtered water daily
- Break up your intake into smaller portions consumed regularly rather than intermittent bingeing or snacking
- Add mineral salts or lemon to enhance absorption and per-meal hydration

With dietary intake optimized along these guidelines, you'll experience increased steady energy levels, cognitive clarity and overall enhanced physical and mental performance across the board.

And when you prioritize quality sleep by avoiding inflammatory and stimulating substances – plus nourishing your mitochondrial function with abundant dietary nutrient cofactors – your daily levels of motivation and resilience amplify dramatically.

Over time as healthy eating practises become ingrained habits, the beneficial impacts compound into truly profound changes to your overall mood, cognition and energy levels. You will progressively experience:

- Increased metabolic flexibility and fat-burning efficiency.
- Balanced circadian rhythms promoting deeper, more restorative sleep.

- Boosted mitochondrial function unleashing more available ATP energy
- Reduced systemic oxidation and inflammation dragging you down
- Enhanced neurogenesis and synaptogenesis fuelling cognitive abilities
- Improved vagal tone and heart-rate variability stabilizing a positive mood

As you strip away inflammatory trigger foods and nurture your entire system with premium nutrition, you will feel the transition from surviving to thriving with abundantly vibrant energy and drive.

The anxiety, irritability and motivational resistance begin shedding away as your body re-establishes homeostasis and starts purring like a finely-tuned machine. You find yourself naturally gravitating towards more nourishing choices and present-moment activities that amplify your blooming zest.

You quite literally become hardwired for operating at a higher level through very building blocks comprising your moment-to-moment physical and cognitive experience. When nourished at a cellular level through conscious practise, vibrant zest, inspiration and drive start overriding any inertia or resignation. Unleashing your fullest human potential becomes an inevitable biological by product gifted through true dietary wisdom.

❑

CHAPTER 17

Exercise Most Days

"The pain you feel today will be the strength you feel tomorrow."

– Unknown

Getting consistent exercise feels like a constant uphill battle against inertia for most people. Your body's prime directive is to conserve energy, so voluntarily expending it through tough physical activity goes against our innate laziness tendencies.

Exercise demands that you repeatedly override comfort zones, summon motivation and disciplined follow-through. You are flexing vital "anti-laziness" muscles with each workout that amplify drive, resilience and general vitality.

On a biochemical level, exercise promotes neurochemical releases while facilitating structural brain changes that improve executive function and fend off apathy or malaise. It is like renovating your body's operating system to run with higher-octane motivation and positive energy.

Mind-Body Benefits

- Exercise promotes mitochondrial biogenesis to generate more cellular energy.

- It increases BDNF levels to improve neurogenesis and brain plasticity.
- Physical activity balances neurotransmitters such as dopamine, serotonin, norepinephrine.
- Anti-inflammatory effects help regulate appetite and improve gut health.
- Improved heart health and blood flow increase oxygen and nutrient delivery.

In essence, structured exercise quite literally biohacks your mind-body system into operating in a more youthful, resilient, and positively-energized state.

Of course, building any new habit carries an unmistakable "activation energy" obstacle for most – which is precisely why consistency needs to be the core priority before optimizing any other variables.

Here is the reality – your body doesn't discern between different workout intensities or protocols. What actually drives training prompts are the signals and patterns you repeat on a regular basis rather than any individual session.

Combatting laziness involves a combination of physical activity, mental stimulation and lifestyle adjustments.

Types of Exercises and Activities

1. **Cardiovascular Exercises:** Activities like running, cycling, swimming, or brisk walking can boost your heart rate and circulation, increasing energy levels and reducing feelings of lethargy.

2. **Strength Training:** Building muscle through weightlifting or bodyweight exercises can improve overall strength and endurance, helping you feel more capable and energized throughout the day.

3. **Yoga:** Practising yoga can enhance flexibility, improve posture, and promote relaxation, reducing stress and combating feelings of laziness.

4. **High-Intensity Interval Training:** Short bursts of intense exercise followed by brief rest periods can rev up your metabolism, increase energy levels, and improve overall fitness.

5. **Group Fitness Classes:** Joining group exercise classes like spinning, Zumba, or kickboxing can provide motivation, accountability, and social interaction, making it easier to stay active and combat or fight laziness.

6. **Outdoor Activities:** Engaging in outdoor activities like hiking, gardening, or playing sports not only provides physical benefits but also exposes you to fresh air, sunlight, and nature, which can boost mood and energy levels.

7. **Mindfulness Practises:** Activities such as meditation, deep breathing exercises, or tai chi can calm the mind, reduce stress, and increase mental clarity, helping you overcome feelings of laziness.

8. **Dance:** Whether it's formal dance classes or just dancing around your living room to your favorite music, dancing

is a fun or enjoyable way to get moving, improve coordination, and elevate your mood.

9. **Pilates:** Pilates focuses on core strength, flexibility, and overall body awareness, which can improve posture, alleviate muscle tension, and boost energy levels.

10. **Circuit Training:** Alternating between different types of exercises with minimal rest in between can keep your workouts dynamic and engaging, preventing boredom and laziness.

Remember to choose activities that you enjoy and that fit your fitness level and preferences. Consistency is key, so aim to incorporate regular exercise into your routine to combat laziness effectively.

So with that in mind, here are some practical tips to make exercise an easy, ingrained daily practise to detox your life of laziness:

- **Keep It Simple:** Don't overcomplicate your workouts. Start with manageable 15-20 minute sessions focused on things like bodyweight/mobility training, walking or gentle yoga. Small steps daily > infrequent heroic efforts.

- **Find Your Whys:** Lack of motivation often stems from not connecting your reasons for exercising. Go deeper than just "losing weight" or appeasing others – anchor into your core driving values.

- **Stack Your Habits:** Design your ideal productive morning by anchoring your workout as the triggering kickoff habit. You will find exercising promotes an upward spiral of making healthier choices all day long.

- **Leverage Accountability:** Workout partners, listings boards or digital coaches provide invaluable outside inspiration and adherence support as you establish your new routine.
- **Make it Fun:** Diversity and variation are key for sustained engagement. Explore new activities or exercise formats you genuinely enjoy rather than subjecting yourself to dread-fests.

More than just unlocking newfound physical capacity and confidence, you will begin feeling sharper and more psychologically centred throughout your entire day. Tasks and challenges that once felt draining or insurmountable will seem to pass with greater ease and focused energy.

And importantly, as exercise promotes independence and self-efficacy, the concept of "laziness" will progressively feel more alien and implausible in your experience. Simply put – you will not stay shackled to physiological and psychological states hospitable for indolence when strengthening and elevating your human operating system.

❑

Chapter 18

Sleep Well

"Sleep is the golden chain that ties health and our bodies together."

– Thomas Dekker

In our hyper-connected, burnout-glorifying culture, sufficient quality sleep has become an endangered species for far too many. Between binge-watching, endless scrolling and the siren call of one-more-thing, we have normalised excessive alertness well into what should be our body's restorative downtime.

But here's the hard truth – when you chronically deprive yourself of the sleep your mind and body so desperately crave, you are essentially rendering yourself in a state of perpetual jet-lag. Is it any wonder fatigue, brain fog and procrastination-fuelling impulses feel like constants when your system is running on empty?

On the flip side, prioritising restorative sleep as a healthy practise empowers you to fire on all cylinders each morning – energised, focused and equipped to efficiently tackle whatever comes your way. It is like gifting yourself a full system reboot and restart daily to approach life with clarity and resilience.

Sleep helps in cognitive and physiological functioning:

- Cell repair, muscle recovery and tissue regeneration process
- Vital hormone regulation like growth, thyroid, cortisol and more
- Memory consolidation and processing of newly learned material
- Immune function, detoxification and inflammatory regulation
- Neurogenesis and neural pathway formation for learning

Sleep truly is your body's ultimate preventative medicine and performance-enhancing super-elixir all wrapped into one. Which is precisely why it should be stubbornly guarded and prioritized like your most precious resource.

Sleep as a Mindful Healthy Practise

- **Environmental Control:** Think like a sleep zookeeper protecting your cave! Eliminate artificial light and blue spectrum exposure, keep your sleep space cool, dark and de-cluttered. Consider blackout curtains, an eye mask, or earplugs if needed.
- **Circadian Alignment:** As diurnal beings, syncing your bedtime and wake times to natural light/dark cycles is vital. Prioritize early morning sunlight, midday brightness and winding down in cosy evening darkness.

- **Pre-Bed Routine:** Habituate a relaxing sequence of rituals each evening to help cue your brain for quality rest. Activities like light yoga, meditation, journaling, bathing or book reading can hit the reset button.
- **Limit Stimulants:** Decrease potential sleep saboteurs like caffeine, nicotine or alcohol as your evening progresses. Avoid any stimulating screen-time for 1-2 hours before bed as well.
- **Temperature Regulation:** Your body needs to drop its core temperature to ease into quality sleep. Paradoxically, slightly cooler ambient room temperatures around 65F can facilitate the process.
- **Sleep Tracking:** To reveal actionable insights into your sleep cycles and energy curves, leverage wearable tracking technology. This data can powerfully inform your personalized optimization.

When fatigue accumulates due to inadequate sleep, your brain begins frantically searching for quick "energy" hits wherever available – junk food cravings, social media dopamine loops, TaskManager multitasking, etc. But maintaining prioritised high-level habits requires calm presence and energy availability – assets abundantly bestowed through quality sleep.

Adequate high-quality sleep is no longer something to sheepishly admit weakness for – but an empowering lifestyle asset to relish and strictly defend from unnecessary compromise.

By shifting your psychology around sleep's preciousness and treating it with the reverence it deserves, you create a positive feedback spiral. Each night of rejuvenating rest begets more motivation, focus and productive action during the day. . . Which then reinforces sound night-time patterns and routines preparing you for another stellar sleep opportunity.

Sound Night-Time Patterns and Routines

1. **Establish a Consistent Sleep Schedule:** Aim to go to bed and wake up at the same time every day, even on weekends. This helps regulate your body's internal clock and promotes better sleep quality.

2. **Create a Relaxing Bedtime Routine:** Engage in calming activities an hour or two before bedtime, such as taking a warm bath, practising gentle yoga or meditation, reading a book, or listening to soothing music. This can help signal to your mind and body that it is time to wind down.

3. **Optimise Your Sleep Environment:** Keep your bedroom cool, dark, and quiet. Invest in comfortable bedding and consider using blackout curtains or an eye mask to block out any external light sources. Ensure your mattress and pillows are supportive and comfortable.

4. **Limit Screen Time Before Bed:** The blue light emitted by electronic devices can suppress melatonin production, making it harder to fall asleep. Avoid using

smartphones, tablets, or computers for at least an hour before bedtime.

5. **Practise Relaxation Techniques:** If you find yourself lying awake with racing thoughts, try deep breathing exercises, progressive muscle relaxation, or visualization techniques to calm your mind and body.
6. **Avoid Stimulants and Heavy Meals:** Steer clear of caffeine, nicotine, and large, heavy meals close to bedtime, as they can interfere with your ability to fall and stay asleep.
7. **Keep a Gratitude Journal:** Before bed, spend a few minutes reflecting on the positive aspects of your day and writing down things you are grateful for. This can promote a sense of calm and contentment, making it easier to drift off to sleep.
8. **Plan Your Next Day:** Taking a few minutes to plan and prioritize your tasks for the following day can help clear your mind and reduce anxiety about the day ahead.
9. **Implement a Calming Night-time Ritual:** Find a ritual that works for you, such as reading a few pages of a book, practising light stretches, or listening to a relaxing podcast or guided meditation.
10. **Avoid Napping Too Late or for Too Long:** While napping can be beneficial, napping too late in the day or for too long can make it harder to fall asleep at night.

By incorporating these night-time patterns and routines into your daily life, you will be better prepared for a restful night's sleep, which can help you wake up feeling refreshed and energized, ready to tackle the day ahead with productivity and focus, leaving little room for laziness to creep in.

In embracing sleep optimization, you affirm the supreme self-care of preparing your most precious instrument – your mind and body – for its highest level of masterful expression every single day.

What could be a more heavy-duty laziness detox than upgrading your core operating systems to run with limitless potential, creativity, perseverance and drive? That is the gift of honouring sleep's rejuvenating prowess as a non-negotiable healthy practise.

❑

Chapter 19

Moments of Bliss

"Almost everything will work if you unplug it for a few minutes... including you."

– Anne Lammot

In our battle against laziness and perpetual quest for optimum productivity, it is easy to start seeing any personal indulgences or leisure activities as weaknesses to be ruthlessly eliminated. But as legendary golfer Arnold Palmer knew well, those minuscule pockets of bliss, relaxation and restorative play are absolutely vital to sustaining your performance over the long haul.

Think of your motivation and energy reserves like a bank account. Each work sprint, productivity burst or goal-chasing pursuit makes a withdrawal of those valuable resources. Without strategically scheduling any "deposits" in the form of recharging and soul-nourishing activities, you will inevitably go bankrupt and end up demotivated on the perpetual laziness treadmill.

But by intentionally peppering in brief "moments of bliss" throughout your day and weeks, you are giving yourself the mental and emotional refreshes required to refill that motivational tank before it runs on fumes. These outlets provide inspired boosts of joy, playfulness and rejuvenation to amplify your well-being and sustain your hustle.

More than just avoiding burnout, carving out pockets of bliss as a healthy practise catalyses peak performance by promoting key **"rest and digest"** states like:

- **Stress Relief:** Overexposure to cortisol and other stress hormones sabotages your cognition, insulin sensitivity and recovery processes. Purposeful relaxation provides antioxidant relief.
- **Neurogenesis:** Generating new brain cells, memory and focus skyrockets in duration proportional to your daily powerdown periods. So does creativity.
- **Embodiment:** Getting out of your head and reconnecting with senses, emotions and experiences beyond just ambition and achievement. Feeling alive!
- **Reframing:** Positive activities disrupt obsessive sacrifice narratives, giving your brain much-needed new references for happiness outside endless striving.

So whether it is 10 minutes of restorative yoga breaths, jamming out to music that inspires you, going for a mindful stroll or savouring your morning coffee – these blissful interludes provide vital rejuvenation to recharge you for your next motivated sprint.

As resolution guru Brad Stulberg says, "Unicorns don't exist, but human beings do. We aren't machines. We are renewal creatures who need to structure our lives for oscillation to live and perform at our best."

However, fully receiving those state-shifting benefits requires making intentional bliss breaks a non-negotiable healthy lifestyle practise versus indulging in them sporadically and haphazardly.

You are proactively scheduling these mini-holidays into your calendar – not guiltily wiggling them in only once burnout strikes. Purposeful pockets of bliss become welcomed rhythms enriching your day rather than deviations or indulgences.

Some suggestions for integrating moments of bliss as a mindful healthy practise:

- **Time-Cube It:** Most find success blocking out periods on their calendar like "10 am Tues/Thurs Bliss Break." Treat it as inviolable as a meeting.
- **Anchor to Habits:** Design blissful activities as rewarding ends to productive windows or habits – example: yoga after morning routine.
- **Stack for Joy:** Combine several blissful activities into one glorious blitz – maybe music, journaling and coffee l on your patio.
- **Change Locations:** Seek out new locations and spaces for bliss-breaks to create fresh mental associations beyond work zones. Parks, gardens, beaches.
- **Schedule Intensity:** Purposefully pursue activities requiring enough physical or mental activation to fully recharge. Hobbies like surfing, archery or dance.

The key is establishing and defending sanctuaries within your week where truly restorative value-aligned joy, playfulness and bliss can flourish without restraint or dilution.

By turning blissful breaks into recurring healthy practises, you create fertile oases that regularly restore your sense of zest, inspiration and childlike enthusiasm. In these blissful pockets, you temporarily shed layers of stress, cynicism and ambition that accumulate from your intense chasing.

You remember what it feels like to be energised and alive beyond instrumental goals, experiencing delight for its own sake. Playfulness returns to greet you like an old friend, reminding you not to grow permanently jaded.

And from this refilled space of peace, beauty and abundance, your highest motivations and aspirations are re-clarified and amplified rather than drained. You recall why you have chosen this challenging path and the powerful impact you are aiming to create.

That is the magic of making bliss a regularly sequenced healthy practise rather than a scarce delicacy. Each infusion carries a compounding effect that reinforces your zest, unique inspiration and perseverance for your true aims.

You come to honour these moments of bliss as holistic performance enhancing interludes rather than indulgent escapes. And carried into your productivity zones, you will find heightened capacities for flow-state magic to transpire:

- Deeper presence and appreciation for your daily activities
- Amplified imagination and creativity to problem solve
- Authentic excitement around new growth opportunities
- Crystal clear vision maintaining your purposeful course

Whereas moments of bliss as random deviations inherently foster guilt and mental whiplash trying to hastily return to taskmaster mode – intentionally practising them as a healthy ritual reinforces themes of reverent dedication and aligned thriving.

These blissful windows become seamless elements of your routine nurturing your highest actualisation as a human being, not irresponsible detours away from the script.

By integrating bliss as a healthy practise, the pleasures become less about stimulation and indulgence, and more about replenishment and inspiration to refuel your personal missions.

Hobbies and creative passions you once abandoned as lesser priorities resurge with vitality not as time-fillers but powerful energizing forces multiplying your drive and determination.

You rediscover forgotten sparks of child-like wonder, unabashed curiosity and playing just for the sake of experience – all amplifiers for your purposeful pursuits when channelled with intention!

And importantly, you become viscerally reacquainted with simple gratitude for the abundance and preciousness of each moment rather than being consumed by the grind or whatever destination is next.

When integrated as a mindful healthy practise, these blissful breaks provide the antidote to ambition's chronic emptiness and void-chasing detachment. They restore wholeness, balance and fulfilment to your heroic being.

With bliss rituals encoded into your operating system, you continually renew access to inspiration and pure beingness beyond any accomplishment metric – the ultimate performance-enhancing cocktail.

In essence, making bliss a sequenced healthy practise optimally balances your striving and achieving with equally powerful pauses of reverent receiving, embodiment and joyful presence.

This interplay births unstoppable momentum fuelled by passion rather than forced self-discipline. It creates the appropriate oscillations for you to thrive as the renewal creature you are designed as, allowing creativity and motivation to effervesce freely.

With these blissful rhythms integrated, your moments of struggle and growth phase naturally alchemize into welcomed aspects of your self-actualization journey rather than perpetual drudgery crusades.

You clear space to celebrate, play and luxuriate in the bliss of wherever you currently reside. . . While simultaneously summoning bottomless inspiration for your next ambitious frontier and level-up.

This is the peak productivity code that lazy patterns can never outcompete or disrupt – seamless cycles of purposeful striving energized by rituals of fulfilment, gratitude and replenishing bliss.

❑

CHAPTER 20

Set Reasonable Goals

"Set realistic goals, keep re-evaluating and be consistent."

–Venus Williams

When it comes to dismantling laziness and achieving big ambitions, realistic goal-setting is absolutely pivotal. Because here is the harsh reality – aiming for the moon while simultaneously hoping to pull it off with minimal effort is a recipe for or achieve it inertia and procrastination to take over.

Battling laziness requires creating an inspired yet grounded blueprint to funnel your motivation into manageable steps and tasks. Attempting to white-knuckle enormous progress in a single burst will quickly drain your momentum reserves, often resulting in burnt-out resignation before any traction is made.

But by breaking down your grandest visions into reasonable, clearly-defined goals that don't overwhelm you, consistent progress becomes viable and energising rather than demoralising. You will summon powerful psychological forces like:

- **Achievement Compounding:** Each small "win" reinforces your self-efficacy and sparks motivation for continued efforts.
- **Growth Encouragement:** Reasonable goals align with your current abilities while stretching your capabilities.
- **Habit Installation:** Consistent action towards reasonable targets grooves productive new routines into your psyche.

That is not to say shooting for the stars is unwise. Not at all! Having a powerful overarching ambition or "prize" providing direction and energy is vital. But then the rubber meets the road by reverse-engineering that big dream into incremental stair-steps aligned with your bandwidth.

For instance, rather than attacking your ultimate vision of say, a successful business full-throttle on day one, you might establish an initial reasonable goal of validating your business idea through market research and customer conversations over the first 3 months.

Or if hoping to finally write a book, your reasonable goal might be a weekly commitment to draft 1000 words rather than expecting the first draft done ASAP. By prioritizing consistency over heroic unsustainable spurts, the incremental results start compounding automatically.

The key is setting reasonable goalposts that inspire you with possibility yet remain plainly achievable through the lifestyle you currently lead. Rather than requiring a fantasy overnight overhaul, these objectives should stretch your current habits just sufficient enough to foster positive tangible growth and deepening skillsets.

Because it is through the by-product of achieved reasonable goals that true personal transformation and upgrades to your capabilities happen naturally.

Define "Reasonable" in Your Terms

For some, a daily reasonable goal might be knocking out a series of targeted tasks before noon. For others, the aim is simply getting out of bed and taking a single concrete action towards their ambition.

The key is selecting goalposts that inspire excitement for the growth but don't feel so ambitious that resistance and avoidance ensue.

Get SMART

Make reasonable goals Specific, Measurable, Achievable, Relevant and Time-bound so they're utterly clear and defined. Avoid leaving room for ambiguous interpretation or finger-pointing that breeds procrastination.

Build Feedback Loops

Create tracking systems and set recurring check-in periods to take stock of your progress. This allows celebrating achievements while also re-evaluating and course-correcting where needed to amplify consistency.

Reduce Activation Energy

The more micro-decisions or friction points involved with achieving your reasonable goal, the greater the tendency for avoidance or abandonment. Design your process for seamless transitions and habit triggers from your current patterns.

Beyond establishing inspiring yet practical goalposts, defining your "reasonable" targets also surfaces deeper self-awareness around where you actually reside in terms of current motivation and discipline.

Often what appears superficially reasonable actually requires an unrealistic lifestyle or psychology pivot that is not accounted for.

For example, a reasonable exercise goal of hitting the gym daily before work sounds perfectly sane in theory, but then runs squarely into obstacles like:

- Not actually being a "morning person"
- Lacking a gym anywhere in practical proximity
- Home responsibilities requiring early availability
- Poor sleep habits sabotaging the required willpower

In cases like this, attaining reasonable consistency may actually point towards more achievable interim goals like:

- Instituting an evening walk routine 3x/week
- Purchasing home exercise equipment
- Addressing sleep patterns through schedule shifts

- Leveraging physical activity apps for routines

You see, the true gold of realistic goal-setting is both the consistent incremental progress made while also building profound self-knowledge and personal accountability. Without these illuminating goalposts, blind laziness frequently takes over.

In shining this light on your genuine starting point, you are able to make the necessary lifestyle modifications to ensure sustainable achievement actually remains probable – not just wishful ambition. Consistent momentum and personal growth become integrated into your reality rather than perpetually aspirational.

Little by little, gradually through sequenced reasonable goals achieved, your self-efficacy and success psychology significantly amplify as your default habits and mindsets re-solidify around execution over avoidance-based procrastination.

And with designed feedback loops to regularly re-evaluate your paths and goalposts, a beautiful ultra-clarity begins automatically emerging:

- You develop a heightened intuition around reasonable personal limitations
- Necessary pivots, corrections or accelerations become obvious early
- Self-forgiveness and resilience grow through transparent self-accountability

This consistent re-calibrating of reasonable goals based on your data removes the guilt and rumination often derailing ambitious-yet-static plans. You engineer self-correcting cycles that propel you into constant growth and actualised achievement rather than listless analysis.

With refreshed reasonable goals continually locking into your line of sight, the psychological states of overwhelm and resignation lose their grip over your psyche. In their place, inspired productivity and consistent incremental progress start asserting as your new normal experience.

And as this empowerment cycle reinforces, you will find bigger and bigger ambitions becoming reasonable horizons for you to aspire towards – aspirations that once would have seemed wildly inaccessible and paralysing.

While never compromising your ability to find self-satisfaction and fulfilment in the present, reasonable goal-setting confers a rocket-esque trajectory for your spiralling motivation, skill acquisition, and self-efficacy beliefs around what you can create.

Each reasonable goal achieved begets new even bigger ones that eventually converge upon your highest wildest imaginings and ambitions. But critically, every step of the way remains grounded in consistent inspired action rather than exhausting your precious motivational capital.

No more stalling on the launch pad awaiting an impossibly perfect opportunity to align. You lift off immediately and iteratively course-correct along the way, amplifying your momentum through every achievement rather than awaiting ideal fantasy circumstances.

It is a feedback cycle that gets utterly and absolutely severed from the tendency for paralysis and laziness. With reasonable goals defining your trajectory, your capabilities and psychology start aligning around what it takes to authoritatively seize your loftiest visions.

So in the fight against laziness, establish reasonable goals as rocket-boosters sequentially lifting your motivation and self-actualisation towards the ultimate destinations that once seemed utterly out of orbit.

Set reasonable goals, and you encode authenticity, tenacity and grit into your lived reality. Keep re-evaluating them as Venus emphasised, and you welcome accountability as an honoured guest supercharging your execution. Stay consistent towards whatever goals reasonably precede you at any given phase, and personal achievement and transformation become inevitable arrivals on your present path.

❑

CHAPTER 21

Create Accountability

"Accountability is the glue that ties commitment to the result."

– Bob Proctor

Let's be real – we are all great and adept at talking about our hopes, dreams, and goals. Daydreaming and fantasising about future accomplishments is probably one of humanity's favorite pastimes. However, there's a vast canyon between wishful intention and actualised results.

Without rigorous accountability practises in place, the temptations and path of least resistance posed by laziness and inertia will endlessly derail your momentum.

Accountability is the glue that ties your commitment to the desired result. By establishing stringent accountability contingencies, you create unwavering incentive structures aligned with your highest aims.

Commitment transforms from an unchecked personal choice into an ingrained lifestyle obligation – one where you are not the only facilitator. Suddenly, you are spliced into a binding agreement with real personal and social consequences tied to your follow-through.

The Power of Accountability

When designed and activated properly, accountability weaves powerfully motivating threads, including:

- **Stakes and Consequences:** Establishing clear metrics that matter to you, along with defined repercussions for dropping the ball.
- **Consistency Commitment:** Putting persistent action and follow-through on your calendar as firm appointments you must uphold.
- **Progress Tracking:** Making achievements, failures, and actual behaviours visible and documented without ambiguity.
- **Outside Support System:** Calling upon motivating partners, coaches, communities, or routines that override self-limiting narratives.
- **Public Commitment Devices:** Pre-committing your intentions and progress to your full social sphere, tying your inspiration to potential impact on others.

Accountability practises become the scaffolding, coach, and sturdy bridge between your aspirations and their embodiment in reality.

The Transformation of Accountability

Consistently embracing accountability as a mindful practise helps rewrite outdated lazy narratives and habituate your success psychology:

- **Installed Integrity Upgrade:** With progress tracking and external commitment devices, your relationship with authenticity transforms. Falling short or making excuses means public fallout.
- **Stakes Raise Self-Respect:** Self-negotiations around motivation wane significantly once tied to tangible social, financial, or status consequences.
- **Inspiration Fortified:** With consistent action and momentum guaranteed by your accountability structures, inspiration continually self-compounds.
- **Psychological Safety Expands:** Grounded by progress data and supportive communities, long-held fears and doubts begin losing their power.

The real magic of embracing accountability is the profound psyche transformation that occurs. These rigorous frameworks reprogram your instincts and associations with what is possible when motivation dips or difficulties spike.

Serena Williams, the tennis legend, is known for her unwavering commitment and accountability. She once said, "One of the most important keys to success is accountability. It is not something you can just talk about – you have to live it every day."

Cultivating Intrinsic Motivation

One of accountability's greatest superpowers is its ability to amplify intrinsic motivation – that fire in your belly stemming from profound personal desire rather than fear or obligation.

As you celebrate goal attainments, you begin palpably owning your inspired potential beyond any societal expectation or risk. This is when the rubber truly meets the road for lasting personal transformation – where intrinsic purpose and empowered work ethic awaken within you to blaze your chosen trail forward.

By rooting accountability as a healthy practise for dismantling laziness, you reinforce your intrinsic identity as someone committed to purposeful perseverance and unwavering resolve – regardless of fluctuating emotions or obstacles.

With airtight accountability frameworks holding you accountable, you transcend the luxury of optionality when inspired action and consistency beckon. Personal integrity emerges as the powerful throughline governing your path.

In this virtuous cycle birthed by rigorous accountability practises, the laziness habit atrophies away, replaced by an addiction to profound growth, resilience, and impassioned results-realization.

The accountability you originally instituted as a mindful practise morphs into awakened intrinsic ownership over your life's trajectory, obliterating any notion of lazy backsliding from your operating system. It is an exhilarating state of being where personal discipline and glorious commitment to your journey are simply givens – your new refreshed default script.

❑

CHAPTER 22

Create an Action Plan

"A goal without an action plan is just a day dream."

– Nathaniel Branden

We have all had those big dreams and lofty goals that we get super excited about initially, only to have them fizzle out over time. Why does this happen? Often it is because we don't have a concrete action plan to turn our goals into reality.

Creating an action plan is crucial for overcoming laziness and actually achieving what you set out or propose to do. Without one, your goals remain vague ideas that are easy to rationalize away or continually put off or delay. An action plan gives you a roadmap to follow, breaking down your big goals into specific, manageable steps. It provides clarity, direction, and accountability.

Think about it this way – if you wanted to take a long road trip, you wouldn't just randomly start driving with no plan or directions, right? You would map out your route, outline where you will stop for gas/food/hotels, and have a rough schedule for making it to your destination. An action plan for your goals is like your road trip itinerary – it lays out and prepares the path to get you where you want to go.

The best part is, crafting an action plan is a remarkably simple process that just takes some focus and forethought. Here are some key steps to create an effective action plan:

1. **Define Your Goal Clearly:**

   What exactly do you want to achieve? Get super specific and clear here. Vague goals like "get healthier" are hard to plan for. Better goals are "lose 20 pounds" or "exercise 5 days a week for 30 minutes." The more precise you can be, the easier it is to map out or plan steps.

2. **Break It Down Into Chunks**

   Look at your overarching goal and break it down into smaller, manageable chunks or milestones. For example, for losing 20 pounds your chunks could be:

   - Lose 5 pounds
   - Lose another 5 pounds
   - Lose 5 more pounds
   - Lose the final 5 pounds
   - Or for exercising regularly, you could break it into 30-day chunks where you exercise 5 days a week each month. Having these bite-sized pieces makes your major goal feel far more achievable.

3. **Outline the Individual Steps**

   For each of your chunks, get granular and list out all the step-by-step actions you will need to take to achieve that piece. For losing 5 pounds, your steps may include:

- Meal prep healthy lunches each week
- Go for a 30-minute walk 5 days a week
- Drink 80 ounces of water daily
- Eliminate dessert and fried foods

Be as thorough as possible here. Look at your goal or objective from all angles and consider all the things you will need to do. No step is too small to include!

4. **Set Deadlines and Schedule**

Now that you have all your steps listed out, it is time to put dates next to each one so you have a schedule to follow. Be realistic here, but also push yourself just slightly out of your comfort zone. Having deadlines creates motivation and urgency.

5. **Identify Potential Roadblocks**

Before finalizing your plan, take a step back and try to anticipate any obstacles or roadblocks that may get in your way. Things like:

- Tempting situations that make you want to slip (like happy hours with friends)
- Negative thought patterns that could derail you (like all-or-nothing thinking)
- Practical hurdles to work around (like an insanely busy week at work)
- The more prepared you are for these roadblocks, the easier it'll be to overcome them. You can then build strategies into your plan to address them head-on.

6. **Build in Accountability**

   Studies show you are exponentially more likely to stick to your action plan if you have some accountability built in. This could involve:

   - Updating a friend/family member on your progress weekly
   - Posting updates in an online community group
   - Having a workout friend or companion to meet
   - Setting calendar reminders to check in on your plan
   - Any method where you have to actively check in and be accountable to someone/something can provide that extra motivational push.

7. **Schedule Plan Review Dates**

   Every few weeks/months, schedule some time to review and adjust your action plan as needed. Goals and situations can change, so being able to adapt your plan is important. Use these review sessions to assess what is working well, what needs improvement, update your steps/deadlines accordingly, and re-commit to the path ahead.

The great thing about having a concrete action plan is that it transforms Your Big Goal from just a wish into a tangible, achievable thing. You now have a clear picture of exactly what needs to happen, when, and what you will need to do to overcome any obstacles along the way. No more guesswork or "I'll get to it tomorrow" mentality.

Does this mean your action plan will be 100 percent perfect and easy to follow at all times? Of course not – there will absolutely still be hurdles and lapses in motivation. That is life! But having your plan in place gives you a sturdy framework to draw energy and clarity from when those inevitable lapses happen. You can get back on track easily rather than having to start over from scratch.

The path to achieving your goals is rarely a straight, seamless line. But with a thoughtful, thorough action plan, that path becomes clearly illuminated with the specific steps, deadlines, and accountability to guide you every step of the way. No more drifting aimlessly – just purposeful movement in the direction of making or transfoming your biggest dreams into realities.

❑

CHAPTER 23

Tech Time-Out (Digital Detox)

"Spend some time disconnected from technology and reconnected with the world around you. It is worth it."

– Germany Kent

In our hyper-connected world, most of us are plugged in to some kind of tech pretty much 24/7. Smartphones, laptops, televisions, tablets – the constant flow of information and stimulation from our digital devices is never-ending. While this level of access and connectivity is incredibly useful (and frankly, pretty amazing), it can also zap our energy and productivity in some surprising ways.

Think about it – how many times have you fallen into a social media rabbit hole, only to emerge an hour later feeling lethargic and unmotivated? Or struggled to focus on an important task because you kept getting pinged by text messages, email notifications, and whatever is trending on Twitter? Maybe you have even experienced the dreaded "burnout" from information overload.

Our brains were simply not designed to be "on" and rapidly shifting focus every waking minute of the day. We need regular breaks from the digital world in order to recharge, regain clarity, and allow our minds to rest. Taking purposeful "tech time-outs" is an incredibly healthy practise that can boost your energy, focus, and overall well-being in some fairly awesome ways.

The Hard Truth About Our Tech Obsession

Straight talk time – when was the last time you were truly unplugged? As in, no phone, email or any tech distractions for an extended period. For many of us, the answer is probably "uhh, I don't remember."

Studies show the average adult spends an astronomical or whopping 7 hours per day consuming digital media. And that's just scratching the surface of how pervasive tech has become. Things like:

- 60 percent of people report struggling with "nomophobia" (the fear of being without your phone)
- 77 percent use a second digital device while streaming TV shows
- The average person checks their phone 96 times per day

Whether we realise it or not, we are glued to our devices in an unhealthy way. And has some alarming impacts on our collective well-being:

- Higher stress levels and anxiety
- Sleep deprivation and insomnia
- Inability to pay attention or be present
- Decreased productivity and motivation

- More loneliness and disconnection (ironic, right?)

The reality is, these gadgets and apps are literally designed to be addictive brain candy that keeps us hooked and constantly hitting "refresh." But our brains can't flourish in that kind of frantic, overstimulated state. We need to build in regular digital detoxes as a core healthy habit.

The Magical Benefits of Unplugging

So what happens when we temporarily cut the cord to our tech world? A beautiful refreshing thing called **mental rejuvenation**. By giving our brains an extended break from digital input, we allow them to reset, recharge, and simply... breathe. Some of the benefits include:

Energy Boost

Feeling that afternoon slump or general fatigue and fogginess? There is a good chance tech overload is a culprit – constantly switching between devices and streams of information is utterly draining for our poor brains. An unplugged break provides a reboot and can leave you feeling refreshed and re-energized.

Improved Focus and Productivity

With no pings or beguiling app notifications to divert you, you are able to bring your full attention and presence to the task at hand. Your brain's ability to go "deep" and do some of its best creative thinking increases dramatically when it is not constantly being disrupted.

Less Stress and Anxiety

The 24/7 onslaught of digital input serves up a continual supply of stressful stimuli for our brains to process – whether it is daunting news headlines, work emails, or just FOMO from seeing friends' Instagram adventures. Unplugging severs that relentless feed and allows stress hormones to reset.

More Connection and Quality Time

When we are absorbed in our devices, we miss out on genuine face-to-face connection with the people around us. Tech breaks make space to be fully present with loved ones, build deeper bonds through undivided attention and create shared "unplugged" memories.

Bouts of Boredom (Yes, This is a Good Thing)

One underrated benefit of tech breaks? They allow our minds to experience boredom...which might just be the secret sauce for sparking creativity, problem-solving, and personal growth. When there is nothing to distract us from our own thoughts, amazing insights tend to bubble up.

If you want to be at your energetic, focused and productive best, hit the reset button on a regular basis through digital detoxes. Going unplugged allows you to refuel your personal battery rather than constantly operating in a depleted state. Think of it as scheduled maintenance for your beautiful brain!

Designing Your Perfect Tech Time-Out

So we have established that digital downtime is crucial... but what is the best way to actually make it happen? The specifics of your tech break can be tailored to what works for your schedule and personal style. Here are some approaches to consider:

Scheduled Blackout Windows

One simple approach is to create recurring tech-free windows each day – maybe a 60-90 minute stretch in the morning before looking at any devices, or an email/social media blackout between 8-10 pm to allow yourself to fully disengage before bed.

App Limits and Website Blockers

Make it impossible to access your biggest digital vices during certain times. Apps like Freedom allow you to block distracting websites and apps with a click. Or you can simply remove easy access to your biggest time-sucks (delete social apps, move video game console to a closet, etc).

Location-Based Detox

Associate certain locations as "no tech zones" to give your mind a break. For example – devices get left in another room or in the car when you are at home after work hours, or put them on airplane mode when out for a walk or hike. Allowing certain spaces and activities to be sacred and unplugged can work wonders.

Activity Swaps

Another refreshing approach is to consciously swap digital activities for enriching analog ones. Instead of plopping or settling on the couch to veg in front of Netflix after work, replace it with reading an engrossing book, going for a walk outside, working on a hobby, or anything that gives your brain a different kind of stimuli.

The Periodic Long Detox

While regular device breaks are ideal, you can also aim for a periodic full "reset" through an extended digital detox. This could be taking one full day (or weekend) completely unplugged each month, or planning a longer stretch (5-7 days) away from it all a couple times a year. It is remarkable how rejuvenating this type of full reset can feel.

Whichever approach you take, make the conscious choice to schedule your tech timeouts on the calendar just like any other important appointment or commitment. Do it as an experiment this week – schedule two 90-minute chunks where you will ditch all devices and unplug completely (no cheating!). Use that time to go for a walk, read, or simply allow yourself to be bored and see what creative thoughts start bubbling up. You may be delightfully surprised at how recharged and sharp you feel!

The digitally-addicted world we live in is incredibly over-stimulating and taxing for our poor brains. We have to be proactive about giving them periodic respite through mindful tech time-outs. Do it consistently, and you will likely notice a significant boost in your energy, focus, happiness, and productivity. After all, even high-performance machines need to power down sometimes to keep operating at their best!

❑

CHAPTER 24

Meditation

"One of the most freeing insights of meditation practise is realizing that the only power thoughts have is the power we give them."

– Joseph Goldstein

Take a second to notice your breath. Inhale...exhale. Mind already wandering a little? That is totally normal! Our human minds are basically like toddlers with endless energy – constantly running from one thought to the next without any real focus or control.

This might seem harmless, but a distracted, all-over-the-place brain has some serious impacts when it comes to beating laziness. When your mind keeps getting pulled in different directions, it is incredibly tough to sustain motivation, concentration and productivity on any one task for very long. That is the major laziness fuel right there. So, how can you build up your mental muscle and gain more control over your easily-distracted mind? Through the simple practise of meditation (admittedly, not always easy).

Put simply, meditating is like doing reps at the gym... for your brain. It is portable mental cross-training that builds core skills like attention, calm and present-moment awareness. And the benefits extend far beyond just feeling a bit more zen – meditation can straight up rewire your brain for better self-control, emotional regulation and conscious decision making.

So what is actually happening upstairs when you meditate? Here's a quick look at some of the good things it is doing for your grey matter:

Thickening Your Brain

You know how exercising a muscle builds it up and adds density over time? Well, studies show that meditating produces a similar effect – actually thickening and reinforcing parts of the brain associated with focus, decision-making and emotional regulation. It is like doing bicep curls for your brain strength!

Pumping the Brakes on Multitasking

The more you exercise your ability to tune out distractions through meditation, the stronger control you have over which thoughts and impulses to pay attention to. No longer is your mind a hamster on a frantic wheel, jumping scattered between tasks and unable to focus.

Stress-Proofing Your Mindset

We all know that stress chemical cortisol is incredibly toxic for motivation and positive thinking. But meditation has been clinically shown to lower cortisol while increasing resilience for handling stressful situations more calmly. Less stress = less fatigue, overwhelm, and general slothery thinking.

Building a Better "Pause" Button

We are often on autopilot, unconsciously giving into cravings and allowing our impulses to dictate our actions. Meditation develops your ability to "push pause" before reacting. This leads to more intentional, examined choices rather than simply falling victim to knee-jerk lazy behaviours and responses.

Boosting Brainpower + Creativity

When your mind gets a chance to relax and just be during meditation, it allows for amazing creative problem-solving, inspiration, and insights to appear on the surface. Many entrepreneurs and artists use meditation as their secret weapon for innovative thinking.

Are you ready to harness all these brain-enhancing benefits of meditating? Here are a few tips to get started on building your own meditation practise:

- Know That It is All Right to Suck at First
- Start Super Small and Be Consistent
- Find What Works For Your Personality
- Schedule Meditation Reminders
- Be Patient and Don't Judge
- Find a Friend, Companion or Community

A daily practise doesn't have to be this huge lofty ordeal. Even spending a few minutes per day watching your breath and allowing your awareness to simply *be* delivers incredible benefits.

Simple Meditation Techniques to Get Started

1. **Breath Meditation:**
   - Find a comfortable seated position and close your eyes.
   - Bring your attention to your breath, focusing on the sensation of air moving in and out of your nostrils.
   - If your mind wanders, gently bring your attention back to your breath.
   - Start with just 5 minutes and gradually increase the duration as you get more comfortable.
2. **Body Scan Meditation:**
   - Lie down or sit comfortably, and close your eyes.
   - Bring or divert your attention to different parts of your body, starting from your toes and gradually moving up to the top of your head.
   - Notice any sensations, tensions, or areas of relaxation without judgment.
   - Breathe into and release any areas of tightness or discomfort.
3. **Mantra Meditation:**
   - Choose a simple mantra, such as "Om," "Peace" or "Relax."

- Find a comfortable seated position and close your eyes.
- Silently repeat the mantra in your mind, focusing on the sound and vibration.

4. **Walking Meditation:**
   - Find a quiet place where you can walk back and forth for about 10-15 paces.
   - As you walk, bring your attention to the sensations of your feet touching the ground.
   - Notice the movements of your body, your breathing and the surrounding environment.
5. **Visualisation Meditation:**
   - Find a comfortable seated position and close your eyes.
   - Visualize a peaceful scene, such as a beach, a garden, or a mountain landscape.
   - Engage all your senses – what do you see, hear, smell, and feel in this imagined environment?
   - Over time, your ability to resist distraction and make progress on your biggest goals will dramatically improve.

Imagine feeling more focused, less stressed, and making conscious, intentional choices rather than just following your whims and auto-pilot tendencies. By meditating regularly, that presence and agency are well within reach.

So no more excuses about meditation being too "out there" or something you don't have time for. Where you allocate your time and attention is what builds habits. By investing even just a few minutes daily into training your mind, you are strengthening your most precious resource for overcoming laziness and achieving what you want in life.

❑

Time Management Techniques

CHAPTER 25

The Eisenhower Matrix

"What is important is seldom urgent, and what is urgent is seldom important."

– Dwight D. Eisenhower

Have you ever felt like your day gets hijacked by a million aimless or insignificant tasks and fires, leaving your truly important goals untouched? You sit down to work on something meaningful, but then a slew of "urgencies" constantly pulls your attention away. By the end of the day, you have spent hours on busywork while your top priorities linger...unstarted.

Sound familiar? Well, my friend, what you need is a simple system for separating the vital from the trivial. And that's where the brilliant Eisenhower Matrix comes in.

What is the Eisenhower Matrix?

Named after the 34th US President Dwight D. Eisenhower, this productivity hack helps you quickly categorize tasks based on two criteria:

1. **Urgency:** Stuff with looming deadlines or crisis-level demands.

2. **Importance:** Actions directly tied to your highest-leverage goals.

   Using these axes, the matrix creates four distinct quadrants to guide your priorities:

   1. Important AND Urgent
   2. Important BUT Not Urgent
   3. Not Important BUT Urgent
   4. Not Important AND Not Urgent

By evaluating where tasks fall, you get crystal-clear directions on where to focus your precious time and energy.

The Four Quadrants Explained

- **Quadrant 1 (Important and Urgent):** These are your highest priorities that need immediate attention, like a tight work deadline. You **MUST DO** these items now.
- **Quadrant 2 (Important and Non-Urgent):** Big rocks like planning goals, exercising, or working on major projects. You should **SCHEDULE** these vital activities before they become urgent fires.
- **Quadrant 3 (Not Important and Urgent):** These are the nagging little tasks that tend to hijack our days – urgent emails, tangential meetings, other people's "emergencies." You should **DELEGATE** or streamline these if possible.
- **Quadrant 4 (Not Important and Non-Urgent):** Pure time wasters like infinite social media scrolling or TV binges. You simply need to **DROP** these from your life.

The beauty of this matrix is the extreme clarity it provides on where to channel your efforts for maximum impact.

A Typical Day with the Eisenhower Matrix

Imagine applying this prioritisation system to your typical day:

- You wake up and review your to-do list through the urgency/importance lens. That report due today? Quadrant 1 – You knock that out first thing.
- Your goal to exercise regularly? Quadrant 2 – You block off time to hit the gym before anything else derails you.
- Those emails about attending an optional meeting? Quadrant 3 – You politely decline or have someone else go in your place.
- That nagging urge to scroll Instagram for hours? Quadrant 4 Time-waster – You delete those apps spartanly till you have crushed your big priorities.

With the Eisenhower Matrix as your navigation system, you simply execute the protocol:

- ❖ Quadrant 1 and 2 activities get handled with laser-focus.
- ❖ Quadrant 3 gets delegated or streamlined.
- ❖ Quadrant 4 gets dropped like a bad habit.

No more procrastination or lazy indulgences in trivial distractions. Those are immediately flagged as low-priority. And you certainly would not let those nagging (but unimportant) Quadrant 3 tasks dictate your entire schedule, right?

Making It Work for You

Of course, prioritising effectively takes practise. You will need to get intimately familiar with your key roles and outcomes tied to Quadrants 1 and 2. And it requires discipline to fiercely protect that focused time from the barrage of seemingly "urgent" distractions.

But the Eisenhower framework provides the simple system to make those judgments cleanly. No more getting overwhelm or analysis paralysis – just quickly categorise tasks and respond decisively!

Here's how to get started:

1. **Map-out Your Goals:** What important activities MUST get done soon (Quadrant 1)? What vital (but not urgent) actions need pre-scheduling (Quadrant 2)?
2. **Audit Your Commitments:** What nagging tasks could you delegate or ditch entirely (Quadrant 3)? Most crucially, what toxic habits, apps, or indulgences can you eliminate as Quadrant 4 distractions?
3. **Implement the Protocol:** With clear priorities defined, you will find it infinitely easier to stay focused while dismissing unimportant demands. Simply consult the matrix, then execute accordingly!

The Eisenhower technique helps quiet the noise and aggravation of constant urgencies, so you can stay calm and productive even amidst swirling storms of tasks. By intentionally investing your time into Quadrants 1 and 2, you will crowd out laziness while accomplishing meaningful results.

The Bottom Line

You are the CEO of your life and attention. Don't let trivial busywork or distractions waste another day while your biggest goals gather dust. Use the Eisenhower Matrix as your prioritisation force field to stay hyper-focused on doing the *important* work – no lazy procrastination, just intentional execution!

With this simple productivity system, you will reclaim control of your time and energy. You will finally gain traction on your ambitious aims while navigating demands with clarity and purpose. Give it a try and experience the power of working on what truly matters most!

❑

Chapter 26

Kaizen's Philosophy

"Perfection is achieved not in a single stride, but in small incremental steps continually revisited and improved upon."

– Masaaki Imai

We live in a world obsessed with massive, overnight transformations. Everywhere you look, it is radical promises – "Lose 30 pounds in 30 days!" or "Get rich with this one weird trick!" While those sound alluring, the reality is that lasting, meaningful progress rarely happens with quick fixes. More often, it comes through *slow, sustained improvement over time*.

The Japanese Way of Kaizen

This ethos of gradual, incremental progress is aptly summed up in the Japanese philosophy of *Kaizen*. Translated as "change for the better" or "continual improvement," Kaizen is about harnessing tiny, consistent adjustments to processes and practises to optimise efficiency and quality steadily over time.

Most approaches push for setting audacious, monumental goals that are hard to sustain. Kaizen takes the opposite view

– breaking efforts down into bite-sized, super-accessible *daily habits and 1 percent changes* that compound massively in the long run.

The Power of 1 percent Better Every Day

On the surface, Kaizen's focus on micro-improvements can seem underwhelming. A 1% optimisation here, a slightly better process there – those don't exactly scream "life-changing" right?

But these bite-sized steps, done consistently over time, unleash astonishingly powerful effects through the magic of *compounding*.

Think about it – if you increased your savings by just 1 percent each day, you would double it in ~70 days. And studies show improving a skill by 1 percent daily makes you 37 times better in a year!

Tiny + Consistent = Massive Gains

Why Tiny Habits Stick Better

When practised over time, Kaizen creates a psychological "hack" – we are much more prone to lasting positive change through small, gradual adjustments rather than radical overhauls.

Grand, sudden shifts trigger resistance and fear, leading us to backslide into old patterns. But tiny 1% tweaks feel painless and non-threatening at first, allowing new practises to form habits smoothly without our brains freaking out.

Once anchored through repetition, even more micro-adjustments can layer on top, continually building momentum.

This ethos of gradual, incremental progress is summed up beautifully in the Japanese philosophy of Kaizen. Originating in post-Second World War Japanese manufacturing culture, Kaizen literally translates to "change for the better" or "continual improvement." And at its core, it is about harnessing tiny, consistent adjustments to processes, methods, and practises to optimize efficiency and quality over time.

Where most transformational approaches meander down the path of setting audacious, monumental goals that are incredibly difficult to sustain...Kaizen takes the complete opposite view. The focus is on breaking efforts down into bite-sized, super-accessible daily habits and minuscule changes that steadily compound into massive results over time. Little by little, gradually step-by-step – a marathon rather than a sprint towards radical reinvention.

The philosophy advocates embracing this journey of marginal gains, making tiny tweaks and course corrections whenever there are opportunities for even 1 percent improvement. Its premise is that the wisdom of experience and insight emerges over time as these small changes gradually become ingrained habits and fuel forward momentum.

Getting in the Kaizen Mindset

Ready to unleash the power of incremental progress in your own life and work? The beauty of Kaizen is just how elegantly simple (yet profoundly effective) it is to practise. Here's how to embrace this philosophy of continual improvement:

Say No to Massive Overhauls

When aiming for transformation on any front – your health, finances, productivity systems, you name it – consciously avoid those herculean overnight shifts that feel radically overhauling. We instinctively resist those shock-to-the-system level changes, almost ensuring they'll never stick long-term. Instead, break big visions down into much smaller pieces to optimize over time.

Focus on Accessible 1 percent Changes

Pick just one or two super-achievable 1 percent optimizations or habit adjustments each week. Make them so easy you can't possibly talk yourself out of them. Ideas like: drinking one extra glass of water per day, saving $5 more per week in your emergency fund, spending 5 fewer minutes on social media. Start with whatever minuscule tweak seems laughably simple, and build up from there.

Eliminate All-or-Nothing Mentally

Banish any perfectionistic, binary thinking around your efforts. Kaizen is the antithesis of all-or-nothing absolutism – it is about non-judgmental, continual course correction. So if you slip up or stumble one day, you didn't "fail" – you simply make another micro-adjustment the next day without missing a beat. Progress, not perfection!

Make Adjustments Based on Feedback

Pay close attention to what is working well and what could use some fine-tuning, no matter how small. The Kaizen process thrives on user feedback and insights from experience. When you notice room for improvement, make your next 1 percent incremental change in that area rather than sweeping over-corrections.

Build Systems and Habits to Automate

Over time, all those little marginal improvements ultimately turn into more optimized routines and habits around how you operate. So build in routines, checklists, and systems that sustainably lock in your incremental gains as new operating norms.

Be Patient and Trust Compounding

The biggest mindset shift with Kaizen is developing enough patience and long-term vision to trust the immense power of incremental gains over time. It can feel excruciatingly slow initially, but momentum compounds exponentially eventually. Stay focused on making continuous strides rather than obsessing over instant results.

Kaizen Every Domain of Life

With health, start with a 10-minute daily walk before bigger fitness routines. For decluttering, spend 5 minutes nightly tidying one area.

At work, refine processes through minor tweaks and feedback. You will soon operate with radically higher efficiency.

Even relationships can optimize through 1 percent more active listening or appreciation per week.

The magic is setting a trajectory for constant, never-ending improvement fuelled by bite-sized steps. No need for jarring, drastic overhauls.

So, where are you feeling stuck in an imperfect status quo despite intending change? Whatever the area, Kaizen is your secret weapon for unsticking yourself incrementally!

Start noticing opportunities this week to course-correct by just 1-2 percent towards your vision. At first, those tiny nudges may seem insignificant. But that slow drip forms an unstoppable current of positive momentum over time.

Don't underestimate what Kaizen's consistent micro-adjustments can compound into. Small steps lead to big, lasting transformations – without the overwhelming struggle of radical overhauls. Embrace continual improvement, one delightfully bite-sized change at a time!

❑

CHAPTER 27

Pomodoro Technique

"You can't make up for lost time. You can only take advantage of the time you have left."

– Michael Josephson

The Struggle with Productivity

Have you ever sat down to tackle an important task, started off focused and productive, but then quickly lost momentum? Those little distractions start creeping in – a quick phone check here, an internet rabbit hole there. Before you know it, you have been "working" for hours with little to show for it.

We have all been there – the frustration of being derailed from our goals by procrastination, lack of focus and poor time management. It becomes a vicious cycle where we avoid daunting tasks, leading to more delays and overwhelm. Not exactly a recipe for feeling accomplished!

Meet the Pomodoro Technique!

But what if there was a simple method to reclaim control over your wandering attention and boost motivation? Here's the *Pomodoro Technique* – an elegant productivity hack based on something as humble as a tomato-shaped kitchen timer.

Developed in the 1990s by Italian software developer Francesco Cirillo, the Pomodoro technique combats wasted time and procrastination by breaking your workday into a series of hyper-focused 25-minute bursts, separated by brief rest periods.

On the surface, using a kitschy veggie timer may seem silly. But the Pomodoro technique activates powerful psychological triggers that systematically help us overcome mental roadblocks to getting stuff done.

Why It Works Like Magic?

Creates a Sense of Urgency: Our brains love rising to achievable micro-challenges like "I bet I can power through this for 25 minutes!"

- **Harnesses Time Batching:** We are less likely to procrastinate when tasks are clearly delineated into finite, purposeful blocks of time.
- **Prevents Burnout:** Our brains can't operate optimally without periodic recuperation. The technique bakes in strategic renewal breaks.
- **Provides Micro-Rewards:** Checking off those bite-sized Pomodoros provides endorphin-fuelled motivation to keep going.
- **Makes You Conscious of Your Time:** No more mindlessly squandering hours! You become acutely aware of how you allocate attention.

How to Get Started

The Pomodoro system is very simple to use – all you need is a timer and some willpower:

1. **Grab a To-Do List:** Identify the tasks you want to tackle.

2. **Set the Timer for 25 Minutes:** Commit to working solely on that task until the timer rings. No distractions allowed!

3. **Mark Your Completion:** When the timer goes off, put a checkmark. Doesn't that feel satisfying?

4. **Take a 5-Minute Break:** Use it to reset and recharge. No work during this break!

5. **Every 4 Pomodoros = Longer Break:** After every 4 Pomodoros, take a 20-30 minute break to align with your brain's natural cycles.

6. **Rinse and Repeat:** For larger projects, break them into chunks of Pomodoros.

By incorporating frequent yet brief breaks, the technique alleviates mental fatigue and renews motivation for the next energized burst. The bite-sized 25-minute chunks make daunting tasks feel more manageable.

Cultivating Laser-Sharp Focus

While straightforward, the Pomodoro technique cultivates a heightened sense of purpose, concentration and achievement around each focused interval. It is almost game-like, challenging you to work against a ticking clock rather than an endless slog.

Studies confirm Pomodoro boosts productivity, reduces distractions, increases perceived time management skills and even lowers anxiety. Using it can help you work faster, sharpen focus, prevent burnout and increase motivation to tackle your priorities.

One key psychological aspect is the satisfaction of quick wins from each completed Pomodoro. There is something gratifying about physically checking those boxes off your list one by one and propelling yourself forward with endorphin boosts.

Over time, starting a new focused Pomodoro becomes its own rewarding habit loop. You will appreciate how much more purposeful you feel compared to aimless work modes.

Taking It Further

You can customise Pomodoro for your needs – some prefer 50-minute intervals, others 90-minute blocks. Or incorporate it into bigger productivity systems like agile project management.

The true gift is how Pomodoro transforms our relationship with time from a reason to procrastinate into a driving force for achievement. By using that humble timer, time scarcity becomes motivating and...even fun?

Give It a Try!

So if you are tired of squandering hours in digital distractions or wasted efforts, give Pomodoro a try this week! Grab a timer and start slicing your to-do list into crisp, 25-minute intervals.

Watch what happens when you attack priorities in those purposeful bursts. Tasks like writing, budgeting, strategising – anything requiring brainpower – will likely flow easier once you settle into Pomodoro's energising rhythm.

It may feel silly or purposeless slaving away against a ticking tomato at first. But you will be amazed at how quickly those deliberate focus sessions become satisfyingly addictive.

By structuring your day into dynamic sprints with rejuvenating breaks, you will gain control over your time, attention and motivation like never before. Make the quirky Pomodoro technique your new productivity secret weapon!

❑

CHAPTER 28

Pareto Analysis

"80 percent of the result comes from 20 percent of the causes. A few things are important, most are not."

– Richard Koch

The Frustrating Productivity Paradox

Ever feel like no matter how hard you try to be productive, something *always* seems to get in the way? You wake up early, all pumped to crush your to-do list, but by noon, an avalanche of emails, meetings, and random interruptions have completely derailed your day. *Again.* It is enough to make you question the point of even trying to stay on top of things, right?

Well, what if there is a simple principle that can revolutionise your productivity by helping you identify and focus on the few activities that truly move the needle?

It is called the **Pareto Principle**, also known as the **80/20 Rule**. And here's the idea behind it:

- *Roughly 80 percent of consequences stem from 20 percent of the causes.*
- This unbalanced pattern shows up everywhere:

- 80 percent of a company's revenue comes from 20 percent of its customers
- 80 percent of a website's traffic comes from 20 percent of its pages
- 80 percent of complaints stem from 20 percent of product issues
- 80 percent of your clutter likely comes from 20 percent of your stuff

Named after economist Vilfredo Pareto, who first noticed this phenomenon in Italy's wealth distribution in the early 1900s, the 80/20 principle reveals an immutable reality:

A minority of inputs tend to have a massively disproportionate impact compared to the majority.

A Game-Changer for Overachievers

For those of us trying to accomplish major goals or maximise our time and efforts, the Pareto Principle is an absolute *game-changer*. It provides a simple framework for identifying your highest-value tasks so you can prioritise them over time-wasting trivial pursuits.

Think about it...what if you could pinpoint the 20 percent of tasks and habits that account for 80 percent of your happiness, health, wealth and overall life satisfaction?

By the same token, how amazing would it be to isolate the 20 percent of distractions and inefficiencies that drain 80 percent of your time and energy?

With the 80/20 rule as your flashlight, navigating life's deluge of inputs becomes dramatically easier. You simply let it expose the vital few priorities truly moving the needle amid the irrelevant ones.

For example:

80 percent of your yearly financial gains may come from just 20 percent of your revenue streams

80 percent of your health struggles could stem from 20 percent of poor nutritional habits

80 percent of your joy and energy may flow from 20 percent of your relationships

80 percent of your frustration could be caused by 20 percent of the browsers/apps you use

With these high-value areas illuminated, you can double down on the vital 20 percent drivers while you eliminate or minimise the unproductive 80 percent diminishing your output.

Auditing Your Life's 80/20 Ratio

So how can you start leveraging the 80/20 Rule for supercharged productivity? Start by auditing various aspects of your life through a Pareto lens:

1. **Take a Time Inventory:** For one week, keep a log of everything you spend time on – work tasks, chores, browsing, exercise, dates, etc. Then identify the "vital 20 percent" where most of your time gets invested.

2. **Map-out Your Money Trees:** Where's the 20 percent of revenue streams producing 80 percent of your income? Or the 20 percent of subscriptions/fees draining your wealth? Know these ratios.
3. **Assess Your 20 percent Relationships:** Which 20 percent of relationships and connections produce 80 percent of your happiness and fulfilment? Ensure that they get adequate time.
4. **Examine Key Performance Drivers:** In any domain, identify the 20 percent of skills and habits enabling 80 percent of desired outcomes – then optimise those relentlessly.
5. **Find the 20 percent of Bad Stuff:** For anything you'd like less of (stress, clutter, conflicts), investigate the tiny 20 percent of inputs fuelling 80 percent of the problem. Then eliminate them!

Solution:

Strip away the trivial many distractions and focus on the vital 20 percent of highest-impact activities.

Working Smarter

While most people operate in a mindset of *more inputs = better results*, masters leverage Pareto insights to isolate the high-leverage 20 percent that achieves 80 percent of what they want. Everything else falls away as low-impact busywork.

You will even identify inputs generating *zero* positive yields – meaning you can cut them entirely with no downside! Getting comfortable with this consistent auditing for low-impact activities while ruthlessly optimising the vital few drivers is the key to operating at your sustainable best.

Now, you might be thinking: *"But what about balance? Won't cutting out the other 80 percent make me too ruthlessly efficient?"*

And it is a fair concern. Once you apply Pareto's lens, there is a temptation to discard anything not appearing as mission-critical.

But the point isn't to abandon balance in pursuit of optimisation. It is about separating the high-leverage activities from the trivial ones, then prioritising where your prime efforts get channelled.

With discipline, applying the 80/20 principle delivers balance and peak performance. The lower 80 percent of tasks doesn't vanish, but rather shrinks to its proper, less-demanding portion of your time and energy. Meanwhile, the vital 20 percent of needle-movers get systematically elevated and compounded.

By studying this pervasive Pareto pattern, you unlock a profound advantage: the ability to reverse-engineer any dazzling result by zeroing in on its core 20 percent of drivers producing 80 percent of the impact. *It is the essence of working smarter, not harder.*

Some Real-World Examples

1. **Software Development:** Microsoft found that fixing the top 20 percent of the most reported bugs eliminated 80 percent of the errors and crashes in their systems.
2. **Supply Chain Management:** Walmart realised that 20 percent of their supplier base accounted for 80 percent of their sales. This led them to prioritise their top suppliers.
3. **Marketing:** A famous example from e-commerce is that 20 percent of an online store's products account for 80 percent of its revenue.
4. **Quality Control:** At Motorola, 20 percent of the company's processes caused 80 percent of its defects.
5. **Personal Finance:** Many find that 80 percent of their annual expenditures come from 20 percent of their spending categories like housing, transportation, etc.

In his book The 80/20 Principle, Richard Koch shares how focusing just 20 percent of his time on the inputs that really mattered allowed him to become a multi-millionaire before age 30. So are you prepared to revolutionise your productivity by focusing relentlessly on the vital few over the trivial many? Then start auditing your life through an 80/20 lens today! I guarantee it will be an eye-opening experience.

❑

CHAPTER 29

Eat that Frog Technique

"If it is your job to eat a frog, it is best to do it first thing in the morning. And if it is your job to eat two frogs, it is best to eat the biggest one first."

– Mark Twain

We have all been there – that one huge, daunting task looming over your to-do list like a dark cloud. Maybe it is a massive work project, dreaded chore or difficult conversation you have been avoiding. This proverbial "frog" drains your motivation, leaving you in a procrastination funk.

Pretty soon, instead of powering through that big frog, you find yourself wasting time on smaller, easier tasks that give a false "sense of progress." By the time you finally muster the energy to start on the dreadful task, you are already exhausted from all the delay and lead-up.

The Simple Solution: Eat That Frog First!

There is a brilliantly simple productivity technique designed to eliminate this inefficient procrastination cycle: Eat the Frog. Inspired by Mark Twain's quote about handling the biggest, ugliest tasks first thing in the morning before anything else.

The method is straightforward:

1. **Identify Your Biggest Frog:** The night before, pinpoint your highest-value, most impactful task for tomorrow – your "frog" to devour first thing.
2. **Eat It First Thing:** Before getting consumed by smaller tasks, dedicate your freshest morning energy to eating that frog. Dive in with no delays or distractions permitted.
3. **Then Everything Else:** Only once the bulk of your biggest frog is conquered do you pivot to tackling everything else.

That is it! By clearing your largest hurdle first each day, you instantly reclaim energy, focus and momentum for the rest of your schedule. No more draining your mental bandwidth by procrastinating on daunting tasks all day.

Why It Works Like Magic

While it is simple, the logic behind eating frogs first is incredibly powerful:

- **Overcomes Activation Energy:** Big tasks have lots of "activation energy" like research and planning that needs overcoming first. Eating the frog first uses your peak morning focus to blast through the inertia.
- **Captures Peak Mental Capacity:** Our prime cognitive ability hits its peak early each morning, making it ideal

for complex "frog" tasks before decision fatigue sets in later.

- **Clears Mental Space:** Once the biggest obstacle is eliminated, your mind operates refreshed and liberated, ripe for flow without that draining "frog-shadow."
- **Fuels Motivation and Satisfaction:** Checking off your #1 task first thing delivers a compounding dopamine rush, improving daily fulfilment.
- **Creates Productive Habit Loops:** The more you "eat frogs" daily, the more hardwired this energizing ritual becomes. You will crave that morning hit of progress!

Instead of dreading that big frog and procrastinating to avoid anxiety, you are now embracing it first thing as your #1 priority with perfect focus and energy. It is a productive-hack against human nature's lazy whims over long-term priorities.

How to Identify Your Biggest Frog

Having trouble pinpointing your top frog each day? Try this:

1. Audit all your commitments across 4 categories of value versus time investment.
2. Religiously prioritize "frog" tasks from the high-value, high-impact category above all else.
3. **Use the Ivy Lee Method:** List your top 5-6 tasks, highlight the #1 biggest priority, and eat that first.

The key is getting hyper clear on your most important task that keeps getting pushed aside, then giving it your sharpest focus first thing rather than wasting that precious morning energy on busywork.

Over time, consistently eating frogs will become a massively energizing habit fuelling intentional focus, clarity and progress. Days will feel virtuous and momentum-driven instead of dreary procrastination slogs.

What If My "Frog" Is Massive?

For extra huge frogs requiring extended work – do your best to make meaningful headway on the ugliest chunk first before pivoting to the next priority. The key is committing to that initial burst of progress on your highest-impact item no matter what each morning.

So whether it is finishing that daunting blog post, a major work project, or an uncomfortable conversation – identify the ugliest frog and eat it first before your day's chaos rains down. Make it a ritual to reclaim control of your time and peak mental stamina for what matters most!

❑

Sum Up

Chapter 30

Wake Up Before It is Too Late

"We are what we repeatedly do. Excellence, then, is not an act, but a habit."

– Aristotle

We have been on quite a journey, haven't we? From diving deep into the sneaky all pervasive psychology of laziness to arming ourselves with mindful strategies – we have covered some serious ground. But now, it is time for the final hurrah – a rousing wake-up call to truly leave laziness in the dust!

Let's do a quick recap: We learned that habits are the building blocks of our lives. Whether they're propelling us forward or holding us back, our repeated actions shape our reality. The good news? We have the power to mold new, empowering habits and bid those lazy ones goodbye.

Throughout this book, we have delved into the various facets of overcoming laziness. Each chapter offered valuable insights and actionable strategies to reclaim our time, energy, and productivity. From understanding the psychology behind our lazy tendencies to cultivating habits that propel us towards our goals, we have embarked on a journey of self-discovery and growth.

Now, as we stand on the threshold of a new beginning, let's commit to integrating these lessons into our daily lives. Let us embrace the power of intentionality, cultivate habits that align with our values and approach each day with purpose and passion.

But remember, the journey doesn't end here. Overcoming laziness is an ongoing process—one that requires dedication, perseverance and self-reflection. As you continue on your path, keep these key principles in mind:

Stay Vigilant

Stay vigilant against the lure of laziness. It may try to creep back into your life when you least expect it, but armed with the knowledge and tools you have acquired, you will be ready to face it head-on.

Cultivate Supportive Habits

Cultivate habits that support your goals and values. Whether it is journaling, exercising, or practising mindfulness, make these habits an integral part of your daily routine.

Prioritise Self-Care

Prioritize self-care and well-being. Remember that you are at your best when you are healthy and balanced, so don't neglect your physical and mental health in pursuit of productivity.

Embrace Flexibility

Be flexible and adaptive. Life is full of twists and turns, and it is fine or acceptable to adjust your plans accordingly. Embrace change as an opportunity for growth and learning.

The Power to Shape Your Destiny

You have the power to shape your destiny. By taking control of your habits, mindset, and actions, you can create the life you have always dreamed of—one filled with purpose, passion, and fulfilment.

Remember, change doesn't happen overnight. It is a journey filled with twists and turns, successes and setbacks. But with perseverance and dedication, we can overcome the inertia of laziness and create a life of fulfilment and joy.

Seize the Day

So, go forth, dear reader, and seize the day. The world is yours to be taken—now wake up before it is too late!

Here's the hard truth: No one will hand you the life of your dreams on a silver platter. It is up to you to craft it, one brushstroke at a time. Fortunately, you now possess the palette of colours and the tools to create a vibrant, purposeful masterpiece.

Laziness is a choice, but so is taking action. Which will you choose? The path of least resistance or the road paved with growth, fulfilment and richness?

So, what are you waiting for? Wake up before it is too late, and start living the life you have always dreamed of!

❑